Hi . . .

I'm Daizy Star, and my life is getting kind of crazy. I'm trying to discover my Star Quality, and I don't have much time because I am getting to the end of Year Six and I really, really need to know what my talent in life will be. I am also trying to learn French, because we are going on the best school trip in the history of the universe . . . ooh la la!

It is good to be learning a language – it takes my mind off Dad's new job, which is seriously dodgy. It's not so much what he is doing – it's what he WEARS while he's doing it. Not good. And, if that's not bad enough, my best friends are growing up way too fast and the idea of secondary school is giving me nightmares . . .

Love, hugs and custard doughnuts,

Daizy Star
(aged 11)

Vin Rouge

Miss Moon
best teacher ever!
Pixie
super-cute little sis!
Welcome to my world!
mad about custard doughnuts...
Daizy (me!!!)
Mum
Dad
works too hard!
gone a bit funny...

Becca
not as scary as he looks
Spike
perfect big sis turned moody goth girl...
most annoying boy in the school...
Murphy
Ethan
my best friends!
Willow
Beth

Books for younger readers

SHINE ON, DAIZY STAR

DAIZY STAR AND THE PINK GUITAR

STRIKE A POSE, DAIZY STAR

DAIZY STAR, OOH LA LA!

Books for older readers

DIZZY

DRIFTWOOD

INDIGO BLUE

SCARLETT

SUNDAE GIRL

LUCKY STAR

GINGER SNAPS

ANGEL CAKE

DREAMS AND DOODLES DAYBOOK

LETTERS TO CATHY

cathy cassidy
Daizy Star
Ooh la la!
PUFFIN

PUFFIN BOOKS

Published by the Penguin Group
Penguin Books Ltd, 80 Strand, London WC2R 0RL, England
Penguin Group (USA) Inc., 375 Hudson Street, New York, New York 10014, USA
Penguin Group (Canada), 90 Eglinton Avenue East, Suite 700, Toronto, Ontario, Canada M4P 2Y3
(a division of Pearson Penguin Canada Inc.)
Penguin Ireland, 25 St Stephen's Green, Dublin 2, Ireland (a division of Penguin Books Ltd)
Penguin Group (Australia), 707 Collins Street, Melbourne, Victoria 3008, Australia
(a division of Pearson Australia Group Pty Ltd)
Penguin Books India Pvt Ltd, 11 Community Centre, Panchsheel Park, New Delhi – 110 017, India
Penguin Group (NZ), 67 Apollo Drive, Rosedale, North Shore 0632, New Zealand
(a division of Pearson New Zealand Ltd)
Penguin Books (South Africa) (Pty) Ltd, Block D, Rosebank Office Park, 181 Jan Smuts Avenue,
Parktown North, Gauteng 2193, South Africa
Penguin Books Ltd, Registered Offices: 80 Strand, London WC2R 0RL, England

puffinbooks.com

First published 2012
001

Set in Baskerville MT Standard 13/20pt
Made and printed in England by Clays Ltd, St Ives plc

British Library Cataloguing in Publication Data
A CIP catalogue record for this book is available from the British Library

ISBN: 978–0–141–33744–9

www.greenpenguin.co.uk

1

Some days are cool, right from the start. It's Friday and the sun is shining and Murphy Malone, who is one of my best friends ever, has bought a bag of custard doughnuts to share on the walk to school. My little sister Pixie skips on ahead, kicking through the fallen blossom in the park. What could be more perfect?

Then I remember that our teacher, Miss Moon, has promised us a surprise today.

I frown a little.

'What do you think the surprise will be?' I ask Murphy, licking the sugar from my lips. 'Something to do with secondary school?'

I hope not. We are in our last term at primary now and our first taster day for Brightford Academy is looming. My best friends Beth, Willow and Murphy are taking it in their stride, but it feels slightly scary to me. I don't like change, and this whole growing-up lark is moving way too fast.

'Stop worrying,' Murphy says. 'We know all about that, so it wouldn't be a surprise. Maybe it's about the Year Six trip?'

'Oh, I hope so!'

The Year Six trip is legendary. Every year, the top class at Stella Street Primary goes away for four whole days of fun. Last year's class went camping in the Lake District. They kayaked and abseiled and it rained so much that three of the tents collapsed in the middle of the night, but they said they had the best time ever.

We turn into the school gates. Pixie runs off to

find her friends, and Murphy and I hook up with Beth and Willow to share out the last of the doughnuts and wonder about Miss Moon's promised surprise. Then the bell rings and we file into class, and my eyes open wide.

The whole place has turned French overnight! A big map of France, a poster of the Eiffel Tower and a flag striped blue, white and red have been pinned to the wall. One desk is covered with a red-checked tablecloth and piled high with strings of onions, garlic, baguettes and stinky cheese.

Miss Moon comes in with a tray of warm croissants and a jug of hot chocolate, and tells us that the first bit of the lesson is to eat breakfast French-style. This is a big improvement on the porridge-and-prunes combo Dad has been serving up lately.

Willow puts her hand in the air. 'Are we doing a project on France, Miss?' she asks. 'That would be seriously awesome!'

'In a way, we are,' Miss Moon says. 'Soon, you will be moving up to secondary school, Year Six . . .'

My heart sinks – the idea of secondary school makes me fizz with excitement one minute and prickle with fear the next.

'It will be a challenge,' Miss Moon is saying.

'There will be new subjects to tackle, and French will be one of them. I thought we would prepare a little. Welcome to French Friday!'

'Ooh la la,' Beth says carelessly, as if Brightford Academy holds no fears at all for her. It probably doesn't – lately, I have been noticing that my friends seem much more confident about the leap to secondary school than I do.

Besides, Beth has actually been to France on a day trip with her mum and dad, which means she is just about fluent in French already. Ooh la la sounds very exotic – Beth says it means 'wow'.

We spend the whole morning learning French, and it's fun. We practise buying baguettes and fromage and oignons, using proper euros as currency and dropping in the occasional ooh la la whenever we can. We learn to count to ten and name every fruit,

vegetable and animal we can think of.

Ethan Miller, the most annoying boy in the class, even finds out the French for football. 'Le football,' he repeats, thoughtfully, which just goes to prove that almost anyone can learn French.

We write our new words down in a special jotter with Le Français written on the cover, which is actually very cool.

'*Très froid*,' I say, testing out the French version of this, and Willow raises an eyebrow.

'Very cold?' she asks. 'What are you talking about, Daizy Star?'

'It means cool,' I tell her. 'Well, sort of. Very cold means cooler than cool, obviously. And I am talking about French Friday. *Très, très froid*.'

'Right,' Willow says.

'I hope you have enjoyed trying out your new language skills,' Miss Moon smiles. 'When you

get to secondary school, your French teachers will be very impressed!'

I pull a face. The first taster day for Brightford Academy is a fortnight away, and I am not sure I am ready. Here at Stella Street Primary, we are Year Sixes, the oldest, wisest kids in the school. Once we start at Brightford Academy we will be the bottom of the heap. It's a scary thought.

'There is one last thing I'd like to talk to you about,' Miss Moon tells us. 'As you know, Year Six always takes a class trip towards the end of term . . .'

Everyone sits up extra straight. The Year Six trip is the big one, and we have been waiting to see what Miss Moon has planned for us. Going on a school trip with your mates has got to be pretty awesome. I'm not sure I fancy soggy sleeping bags or dangling from a rope in the driving rain, but being with your very best friends, eating custard doughnuts at midnight and vowing to stick together through thick and thin would be the kind of thing you'd never forget.

'I wonder where we'll be going this year?' I whisper to Beth and Willow. 'I'm not sure if Miss Moon is a tents-and-kayaking kind of teacher . . .'

An idea begins to unfurl in my brain, a crazy idea, an impossible, wonderful one. French Friday. Supposing it isn't just about helping us with our secondary school lessons?

No, even Miss Moon couldn't be quite that amazing. Could she?

'This year, Class Six, I thought we'd try something different,' she is saying. 'Something special. I have talked to Mr Smart, the head teacher, and he is a hundred per cent behind me. He thinks, as I do, that you are a very special year group, and could rise to this challenge very well. You are mature, trustworthy, reliable and eager to learn . . .'

I glance at Ethan Miller, who has ducked down behind his desk and is secretly applying gobbets of shimmery hair gel to his already vertical fringe. He is the kind of boy who likes

to think he has whole crowds of girls crushing on him, which just goes to prove that he is actually not very bright. Although Beth and Willow do seem to think he is cute, that can only mean one thing. They need an urgent trip to the optician.

I am not sure if Ethan is mature, reliable or eager to learn, but I like the fact that Miss Moon can always see the best in people. She has even given Ethan Miller the coveted Star of the Week award once or twice, which is once or twice more than me. Not that I am the kind of person to hold a grudge. Obviously.

'This year's trip could be the most exciting ever,' Miss Moon says. 'I have checked out prices and travel and places to stay, and drawn up a list

of activities. It won't be much more expensive than the camping trips were, and it would be an amazing opportunity for you all . . .'

I think I might explode any minute now, unless Miss Moon spills the beans on our Year Six trip.

'Where are we going, Miss?' I plead. 'You have to tell us!'

'I will, Daizy,' she smiles. 'You'll all be given a letter and some forms to take home to your parents. Thank you for working so hard this morning, and making French Friday so much fun. I hope you'll keep on working at your French because in June we will be going on the trip of a lifetime . . . Year Six, I am taking you to Paris!'

Across the table, Beth and Willow meet my gaze, eyes shining, and my best boy-mate, Murphy Malone, is grinning with delight. My heart thumps. I can picture us now – me, Murphy, Beth and Willow,

posing for pictures at the top of the Eiffel Tower. How totally, awesomely cool would that be?

Paris. I am so excited I think I might faint.

'Ooh la la,' I whisper.

2

Paris! I can hardly believe it. I have never been abroad, not ever. Last year we had a day trip to Eastbourne and there have been a few caravan holidays at drizzly British resorts in the past, but money has been so tight lately that treats have been right off-limits.

There is no way we'll be going anywhere exciting this summer because Dad is having a mid-life crisis and has chucked in his job as a geography teacher to follow his dreams. Mum is working double shifts at the hospital to try and make ends meet, so this trip is my one and only chance to do something cool.

'Do they have mermaids there?' Pixie asks as

we set the table for tea. 'French ones?'

'I don't think so,' I frown.

'You're so lucky,' my big sister Becca sighs. 'Paris is the city of romance.'

'I am not looking for romance,' I say firmly. 'Or mermaids. I am just looking for fun with my friends, and chocolate croissants. And possibly one of those berets everyone seems to wear, because they are *très, très froid*.'

Dad sets down a pan of lentil stew and Mum pours out juice, and everyone sits down to eat.

'So,' I blurt, launching straight into it. 'Can I go to Paris, please?'

That gets Mum and Dad's attention. 'Paris?' they echo.

'For the Year Six trip,' I explain. 'In June. We had a letter about it today. Miss Moon says it will improve our French and we will learn about culture and art and history. We will get to eat croissants for breakfast. And it's got to be better than dangling from a rope in torrential rain, right?'

'Er . . . right,' Dad says uncertainly. 'Lovely, Daizy. But how much is all this going to cost?'

'Cost?' I frown. 'You can't put a price on learning, Dad! This trip is the chance of a lifetime!'

'It's a bargain,' Mum says, scanning through the letter. 'The trouble is, Daizy . . . well, we are seriously short of cash right now. Your dad isn't working and I'm having to cover the mortgage and the bills on one salary. Becca needs a new coat, Pixie needs shoes and you need a whole new uniform for when you start at Brightford Academy. I'm not sure we can manage an overseas trip at the moment, on top of all that.'

My whole world crumbles. I should have thought of this – I know we don't have money to spare right now, but I didn't realize just how bad things were.

Disappointment lies cold and sour in my stomach. Or perhaps that's just the lentil stew.

'Please!' I beg. 'I have to go! I just have to!'

I have never missed a school trip before. Of

course, past trips have usually involved a bus ride to the city farm or a day mooching around a museum full of dusty old relics. I would have missed every single one of them if it meant I could go to Paris.

'I'm not saying you can't go, Daizy,' Mum sighs. 'I'm just saying that it might be tricky. We're struggling as it is, and losing the car was the last straw . . .'

I raise an eyebrow. We didn't exactly 'lose' the car. Dad parked it on a beach a while ago and the tide came in and flooded it with saltwater, seaweed and crabs. Dad bought a rickety old van to replace it, but it's such a wreck it doesn't actually work yet.

'I've got seventy-three pence in my piggy bank,' Pixie says helpfully.

'It's not really enough, Pixie,' Dad sighs. 'Perhaps if we cut back a bit? Sell something?'

My sister Becca rolls her eyes. 'What are you

going to cut back on?' she asks. 'We're already surviving on lentil stew. What's next? Are you going to stop my violin lessons or Pixie's swimming club?'

'It won't come to that,' Dad says. 'We are just watching the pennies, that's all. It's good for our health as well as our finances!'

'Lentil stew is not good for my health,' Becca says darkly. 'Besides, I haven't noticed you cutting back, Dad. You bought all those horrible bits of engine for the van the other day, and now they are strewn all over the garden because you won't admit you don't actually know what to do with them!'

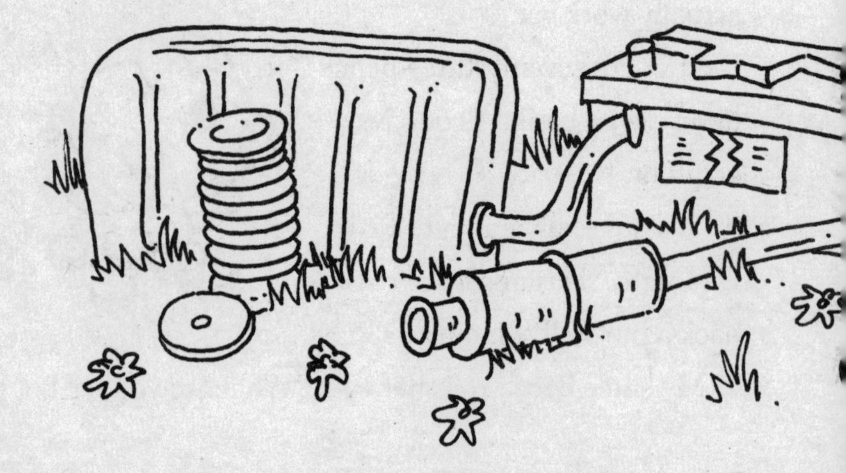

'I do!' Dad argues. 'These things take time, that's all. I have plans for a brilliant new business, and in a couple of months –'

'Dad!' I wail. 'It has to be now! The forms have to be signed and the money handed in because we are going in June. That's only six weeks away!'

Mum rolls her eyes. 'Daizy, don't worry . . . I know how much this trip means to you. I know the last few months haven't been easy. You're a good girl – of course you can go on the Year Six trip. I'll take on some extra shifts at the hospital to cover the costs.'

My heart does a double backflip, then crashes abruptly.

Extra shifts? Mum has already taken on more hours since Dad quit his job. She always looks tired, lately. I am not sure I want her to work more shifts, even if that does mean I can go to Paris. It doesn't seem right.

I look at Mum and then, slowly, I look at Dad. I notice that Mum, Pixie and Becca are all looking at him too.

'What?' he protests. 'What have I done now?'

'You packed in your job for no good reason and money has been short ever since,' Becca says sternly. 'Mum has been working extra hours for ages now to try and keep us afloat, while you just dream up one crazy idea after another. She can't do any more, it's wearing her out as it is! You have to stop this stupid mid-life crisis, Dad. It's not fair on any of us!'

He looks baffled. 'I agree that your mum is working hard enough already. But I have big plans! When I get the van fixed up I will launch my new business!'

Outside the window, the van, a rusting heap

of metal tied together with string and gaffer tape, is slumped on the driveway in a puddle of engine oil. I try to smile, but I feel like crying.

Unless Dad's new business is scrap-metal dealing, things are not looking good.

'I'm going to turn it into a mobile eco-workshop to spread the word about green issues,' Dad says. 'I'll tour local schools and community centres, showing people how to compost and recycle. It could be a real moneymaker!'

'I seriously doubt it,' Becca huffs.

'Mike,' Mum says patiently. 'Launching a business takes time. Daizy needs to hand in her

forms and make the first payment next week. Perhaps we could sell the van?'

'I'd rather not,' he frowns. 'Besides, I'm not sure anyone would actually buy it. I reckon that, in time, my business idea will take off . . .'

Any last fragments of hope that I can go on the school trip begin to wither and die. At this rate, I may still be dreaming of Paris when I'm old and grey. Mum rolls her eyes, defeated, but

my big sister doesn't give up that easily.

'I've got a better idea,' she says. 'It's simple, Dad. We've had enough of your crazy plans to last a lifetime, and right now, Daizy needs you. Why don't you just get a JOB?'

Dad looks astonished, as if the thought has never occurred to him before, but he sees my hopeful face and squares his shoulders bravely.

'Yes,' he says. 'A job. You know . . . I might just do that!'

3

As the week wears on, it is clear that Dad is not planning to dig out his suit and go back to his old job teaching geography at Green Lane Community School. He has other ideas, and they are very, very scary.

'I can't expect to pick up a teaching job at the drop of a hat,' he says, filling out endless application forms. 'It makes more sense to broaden my scope a little.'

'You ditched your job at the drop of a hat,' Becca points out.

'That was different,' he huffs. 'I am looking for new challenges now. Eco-friendly career paths.'

I shuffle through the application letters.

'Wildflower Meadow Manager?' I read aloud. 'Compost Consultant? Yurt-maker?'

'These are not career paths,' Becca snorts. 'They're dead ends. They won't make enough money to send Daizy to France. Get real!'

'Relax,' Dad says. 'I will find a job, and Daizy will go to Paris. Trust me!'

The problem is that these days, I'm not sure if I do.

When he is not job-hunting, Dad works on the van. The creaking back doors are patched and oiled and the spluttering exhaust pipe replaced. Sprayed a glossy green, the van looks almost respectable, even if it does stink of chips every time Dad starts it up.

'It runs on recycled vegetable oil,' Dad explains cheerily. 'Genius, huh? It's going well now, and I'll need something to drive myself to interviews in, won't I?'

'If you actually get any interviews,' Becca says harshly.

I am not holding my breath. My forms for the

Paris trip are still clipped to the kitchen pinboard, unsigned. By the time our second French Friday rolls around, everyone else has returned their permission slips, and when Miss Moon asks about mine I have to pretend I've forgotten them.

I don't want to tell Beth, Willow and Murphy that I might not be going. I don't want to admit that, not even to myself.

'It might be our last time all together as a group,' Beth sighs. 'At secondary school, we will be divided up into classes with kids from other schools. We might forget about each other –'

'We won't!' I argue, alarmed. 'We will be friends forever!'

'I hope so,' Beth says. 'But things change, don't they?'

I bite my lip. I do not want things to change, especially not like that. It is bad enough that Beth and Willow seem to be growing up faster than me, getting all mushy over boys and interested in short skirts and lipgloss. I can just about handle that, but being in different classes too? What if we just drift apart until we are practically like strangers? That would break my heart.

'I don't want that to happen,' I whisper.

'Well, nor do I, obviously,' Beth shrugs. 'I'm just saying . . . it could. We should make the most of the Paris trip!'

'I plan to,' Willow smirks, with a sidelong glance at Ethan Miller.

'Me too,' Beth grins. 'Don't worry, Daizy! Whatever happens, we'll always have Paris!'

Except that maybe I won't.

I try to visualize me, Beth, Willow and Murphy posing for that photo at the top of the Eiffel Tower, but I just can't do it. What if I'm not in the picture at all? Not even on the trip? Things could change fast once we get to secondary school, as Beth pointed out. The Paris trip really could be our last chance to be together, and I might not even have those memories to look back on.

I secretly look up the French word for 'sad' in the class English–French dictionary. It turns out that I am feeling *très, très triste.*

When I get home on Tuesday after taking Pixie to her swimming lesson, there are balloons tied to the gatepost. My heart leaps. Has Dad managed to land himself an interview – or a job?

Inside, Becca is smiling as she sets the table.

'I like the balloons,' Pixie pipes up. 'Are we celebrating?'

'We certainly are,' Mum grins. 'Your dad had an interview today . . .'

'I'm proud to announce that I have a new job!' he announces. 'I am the new Executive Assistant at the Squirrel & Lentil Wholefood Café! You, Daizy Star, are going to Paris!'

He takes the form for the trip from the kitchen pinboard and signs the permission slips with a flourish, handing them back to me along with a cheque for £50.

My lips twitch into a smile, then widen into a grin, until my whole face is beaming.

'Ooh la la!' I say, laughing. 'That's brilliant, Dad!'

Later, as we sit round the table trying to eat watercress and wild garlic stew with mashed parsnip, I can't help thinking that four days away from Dad's evil-smelling, sludge-coloured inventions will be very welcome indeed. Becca chucks down her spoon.

'Disgusting,' she declares. 'I'm not eating it.'

'Mike,' Mum says gently. 'This might be a little exotic for the girls. How about we just fix ourselves some bread and cheese?'

Dad frowns. 'No cheese,' he says.

Mum raises an eyebrow. 'That's funny, I bought a big block of Cheddar just yesterday! I suppose I could make an omelette . . .'

'No eggs,' Dad says.

'No eggs?' Mum echoes. 'We had a dozen free-range ones in the fridge!'

Dad looks shifty. 'I gave the eggs and cheese away,' he mutters. 'They weren't suitable.'

'Suitable?' Mum repeats. 'SUITABLE? Mike, are you telling me you gave fresh food away when we are scrimping and saving every last penny? Are you crazy?'

'Not at all,' Dad promises. 'It's because of my new job. The Squirrel & Lentil is a vegan café – I thought we should all eat vegan too, as a show of solidarity.'

Mum rests her head in her hands.

'What does "vegan" actually mean?' I ask.

'No meat, no fish, no eggs, no cheese, no butter, no cream, no ice cream,' Dad explains. 'No animal products at all.'

'No way,' I say weakly.

'I want to embrace the whole vegan lifestyle,' he says. 'They've asked me to lead a new campaign to make the Squirrel & Lentil a household name in Brightford!'

'Great,' Becca snarls, pushing her dinner away.

Dad sighs. 'Girls, this is important to me. I believe in my new job and it would mean a lot to me to have your support. Things have been tricky over the last few months. I just want life to get back to normal!'

I bite my lip. Is Dad's mid-life crisis over? Maybe he really is ready to shelve the mad plans of the past. No more leaky, half-built boats, no more plans to farm nettles on the Isle of Muck or emigrate to sub-Saharan Africa. He has a job again, and though I am not keen on the vegan plan, surely that can't last for long? Maybe, finally, Dad is coming to his senses?

'We all want life to get back to normal,' Mum says.

'And we do support you, Dad,' I chip in.

He laughs. 'Thank you, Daizy! I knew you'd understand. Part of my new job is to help make vegan food cool, and I had a great idea for getting kids to do just that. Shall I show you?'

'Er . . . sure,' I shrug. 'Go for it!'

He strides from the kitchen and into the hallway. 'It's a simple idea, but effective,' he calls through. 'Once people see this, they will get the healthy-eating message, loud and clear. The Squirrel & Lentil will be unforgettable!'

The kitchen door swings open again and a huge, furry, ginger squirrel appears. It has enormous woolly thighs and tufty orange ears, and a gigantic curly tail that must have some kind of metal frame inside because it stands upright all on its own. The squirrel is wearing a checked apron and grinning horribly in a very familiar way.

'Dad?' I whisper.

'Mike?' Mum gasps.

A muffled voice comes from within the ginger fur.

'The café is hoping to attract a new, younger crowd.' Dad explains. 'And with my help, soon kids will be choosing a trip to the Squirrel & Lentil instead of McDonald's!'

Becca puts her head down on the table, despairingly, and Pixie starts to cry as Dad waddles into the kitchen and dances round the table, his curly tail swaying and his ears twitching. My dad has landed himself a job as a giant red squirrel with a checked apron and a liking for mashed parsnip.

It is lucky I am going to Paris because, let's face it, I won't be able to show my face around here for much longer.

The more I learn about France, the more convinced I am that it is actually my spiritual home. What if there was some kind of mix-up at the hospital when I was born and I am actually the love-child of a Parisian actress and a starving poet with a beret and a striped T-shirt? I can just imagine the two of them sipping their café au lait at a pavement café on the banks of the River Seine while I eat a chocolate croissant and look sweet. At the moment it feels much more likely than me being the offspring of a nurse and a squirrel.

I am counting down the days until the trip. It is good to have something cool to think about

because it stops me stressing about the taster day for Brightford Academy, which is sneaking up fast – I can't believe it's next week. I cannot say I am looking forward to it. I can't imagine myself at secondary school at all. Whenever I try to imagine it, my mind goes blank, like a computer screen when the whole system has crashed and died.

I am not nervous so much as terrified.

What if I get lost trying to find my way around? What if the work is too hard? What if somebody asks me if my dad is a giant red squirrel? I can think of 101 things that could go wrong.

My friends, by contrast, are irritatingly chirpy about it. Beth is looking forward to flirting with a whole new crop of cute boys, while Willow, who has an older sister at Brightford Academy, starts telling us horror stories of tough kids who lurk in dark corners ready to scare unwary Year Sevens.

'She's joking,' Murphy tells me. 'Definitely. Maybe. I hope . . .'

I am not so sure.

By contrast, I feel drawn to Paris. I am drawn to it the way an artist is drawn to paints and canvas, the way a musician is drawn towards violins and xylophones, the way Murphy Malone is drawn towards custard doughnuts.

No wonder I haven't been able to find my star quality in life – I've been looking in all the wrong places. I was never going to find my talent, my destiny, in a place like Brightford, where giant-sized squirrels roam the streets and deeply annoying boys like Ethan Miller are considered to be cute. No – I have a feeling I will find my star quality in Paris.

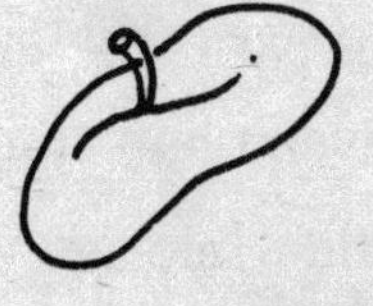

I am destined for treelined boulevards and baguettes and bicycles and berets. I can see myself in an attic apartment with a view of the Eiffel Tower, living a bohemian life with poets and artists and fashion designers and large quantities of chocolate croissants.

I wouldn't swap my real family for anything in the world, but there is nothing like discovering that your dad likes dressing up as a giant red squirrel to make you think.

Days slide by and I still haven't told anyone at school about Dad's new job. They wouldn't understand – even I don't, not really.

'I don't mind too much about not eating sausages and bacon any more,' I tell Dad. 'And I haven't had chicken since we had hens as pets a little while ago. But I don't see why we can't have cheese on toast any more, or boiled eggs, or hot chocolate.'

'Vegans take their nourishment purely from plants and nuts and grains,' Dad explains. 'We are living lightly on the earth!'

It is hard to take this kind of speech seriously when the person delivering it is wearing a fluffy squirrel suit.

'Why don't you bring some of your friends into the café for a carrot and beansprout smoothie after school?' he suggests.

'No!' I say, horrified. 'We are all too busy learning French and packing.'

'You're not going for weeks yet,' Dad frowns.

I promise to think about it, but the truth is I would rather die than bring my friends to the Squirrel & Lentil Wholefood Café. They'd hate the food and I am pretty sure they would laugh at Dad. I can't let that happen. Willow's dad is a doctor and Beth's dad is a plumber and Murphy's dad works at B&Q. None of them have to wear a furry squirrel suit to work.

No, Dad's job must remain secret.

'You could always pop in by yourself,' he prompts. 'Or with your sisters. I can do you a family discount! The Squirrel & Lentil is on Granary Lane . . .'

'I'll remember that,' I say politely.

I will. I will make sure I stay well away from Granary Lane, for the rest of my life, if need be. Paris should be a safe enough distance – it's a pity I can't emigrate right now because it would save me the anxiety of keeping a lookout for Dad in his squirrel suit, cycling to and from work every day. Sometimes, he drives the van, and that is slightly better – except that he has stencilled The Squirrel & Lentil Wholefood Café on the side, along with a large picture of a red squirrel eating an acorn.

'It's good advertising,' Dad explains. 'They want me to take the healthy-eating message out on the road. Go into schools and use my teaching skills to give educational talks and workshops. Show kids that dandelion and tofu burgers are cool!'

'But they're not,' Pixie says, puzzled. 'They are disgusting!'

'Healthy eating can be fun,' Dad insists. 'You'll see. I could ring your school and ask if they'd like me to come and do a workshop on making prune and parsley flapjacks –'

'No!' I cut in. 'We have very healthy food already at Stella Street Primary. We have lentil stew and . . . er . . . kidney-bean custard . . . all the time. So, there is no need for you to come, is there, Pixie?'

My little sister shakes her head, wide-eyed. 'No,' she whispers. 'Not ever!'

'No?' Dad asks, crestfallen. 'I could make it really fun and funky?'

Why do the words 'fun' and 'funky' strike fear

into my heart? If Dad actually came into Stella Street Primary wearing his scary squirrel suit, my life would be over.

I think I will feel much safer when I have put the English Channel between us, for a little while at least.

5

It's Monday and the dreaded taster day has dawned. We set off for Brightford Academy after registration. It is just four streets away, so Miss Moon and the classroom assistants take us there on foot. Beth and Willow are practically hyper, laughing, giggling and winking at Ethan Miller every chance they get.

'I cannot wait to be at secondary school,' Beth declares. 'Do you think we'll be allowed to wear lipgloss and eyeliner?'

'They are quite strict on uniform,' Willow informs us. 'But my sister rolls over the waistband of her skirt a few times, to make it shorter . . .'

'And there's a girl in the sixth form with

purple hair,' Murphy chips in.

'Awesome,' Beth sighs. 'I am so ready for short skirts and purple hair. Seriously, Stella Street Primary is just so babyish these days . . .'

I am silent. Am I the only one who likes things the way they are? I'm not sure that I am ready for secondary school – it sounds way too grown-up. From what I have seen, growing up is nothing but trouble. Look at Beth and Willow, going all mushy over Ethan Miller. Look at my big sister

Becca. One minute she is a violin-playing maths geek and the next she is a full-on Goth, complete with a boyfriend called Spike who has green hair and a pierced lip. It seems to me that growing up is all about exams, hormones, hair dye and heartbreak. I drag my feet, dropping behind a little, and Miss Moon falls into step beside me.

'Excited, Daizy?' she asks.

'Not really,' I admit. 'I'm not sure I am ready for this!'

'You'll be fine,' my teacher says. 'You are an amazing girl, and at Brightford Academy you'll learn to spread your wings and fulfil your true potential!'

I doubt it, somehow. After months and months of trying, I haven't managed to win Miss Moon's special Star of the Week award, so I can't be all that amazing, can I? And I am still a million miles away from finding my star quality. Miss Moon says everybody has one, but even though I'm pinning my hopes on Paris, sometimes I am not so sure I do. A while ago, I thought I might

be the first pre-teen supermodel, but that didn't work out; before that, I tried my luck at rock stardom by forming a thrash-punk-metal band with my friends, but that went kind of pear-shaped too.

Perhaps I don't actually have a star quality? I may be destined to be dull and ordinary and average at everything, for the rest of my life. It's a very depressing thought.

'Give it a chance, Daizy,' Miss Moon smiles. 'The taster day is all about helping you to feel ready. You'll love it, Daizy, trust me!'

I don't love it, though, when we reach Brightford Academy and walk up the big steps and into the entrance hall. Miss Moon goes to the reception desk to let them know we are here, and suddenly a bell rings. Kids appear from every direction, big noisy kids, shoving, laughing, wearing the black and red uniform and carrying giant rucksacks and school bags. They look very grown-up, even though they don't act it, and they are all in a hurry.

I am silent now, feeling way out of my depth, as well as very small and very young. My friends seem to be coping better. Beth is giggling and clinging on to Ethan Miller; Murphy is trying to act cool; and Willow has morphed into someone loud and show-offy and almost as scary as the big kids. She tells us we'll have to get used to this kind of thing if we want to survive at Brightford Academy.

I am not sure I will ever be able to do that.

The crowd thins and finally vanishes, and Miss Moon returns with Mrs Shine, the head teacher.

'Welcome to Brightford Academy!' she says. 'It can be a bit chaotic at lesson change, but don't worry, you'll get used to it! We have a busy day planned for you. First of all, some refreshments while I tell you all about your new school!'

Miss Moon and the classroom

assistants wish us luck, and we file into the library, a light, airy room filled with books and computers, with amazing student artwork on the walls. We take chocolate biscuits and paper cups of squash and sit on bright beanbags and cushions while Mrs Shine talks.

She tells us that we are bound to feel a little nervous about starting secondary school, that everything must be new and strange, but that we will soon get used to it. She tells us about all the new lessons we'll have, from science and CDT to drama and dance. She makes it sound almost exciting.

'I'm going to take you on a tour of the school,' Mrs Shine explains. 'Then you'll have some taster lessons in French and science. Does anybody have any questions?'

Beth asks if lipgloss and eyeliner are allowed (they aren't) and Murphy Malone asks if there are any after-school clubs (there are, dozens, and they sound cool).

Ethan Miller asks about the football team, and Mrs Shine says that the Brightford Academy team has won lots of cups and plaques and is always looking for talented players, and Ethan looks so happy you'd think he had just been signed for Man United.

I put my own hand in the air.

'Miss?' I ask, in a small, shaky voice. 'How do you decide who goes in which class? Will we be separated from our friends?'

Mrs Shine smiles. 'We have found over the years that our students work their best when they are happy,' she tells me. 'For that reason, we always try to put new pupils with their friends. We work with your primary class teacher to find the right mix. And, of

course, you'll make lots of new friends too!'

'See,' Beth whispers. 'Nothing to worry about!'

I feel a little bit better, but still, I stick to Murphy, Beth and Willow like glue as we are shown around the school. It all seems so huge and so strange, from the cavernous assembly hall to the super-cool art studios, the shiny new science labs to the rolling sports fields.

It all looks great, but I can't imagine ever being able to find my way around without a map or some kind of personal satnav. I can't imagine ever feeling relaxed or comfortable here. I can't see myself fitting in at all.

We eat our lunch at a long table in the modern cafeteria. The food is fine, but the place is crammed with noisy students milling around and I feel scared, small, lost. I forget to help myself to water or fruit juice and there is no way I dare go back up to the counter to get it. I stare down at my macaroni cheese sadly, my stomach in knots.

Beth and Willow are still acting all weird and out of character. Are they anxious too, or is this how it will be from now on? The teen mags Becca reads talk about friends drifting apart during the growing-up years. Is that what will happen to us?

'Hey,' Murphy says, nudging my arm, 'd'you think they do custard doughnuts on special occasions?'

'Probably not,' I sigh.

'Just as well I bought emergency supplies then,' he grins, handing me a sugar-dusted doughnut under the table. 'Thought it might help.'

I bite into the sweet, doughy treat, smiling, and Murphy offers a doughnut to Beth and Willow. Their loud, flirty act begins to slip. Soon we are joking around and the fear and worry slowly lift away.

I begin to think that I might just be able to handle secondary school, as long as I have a constant supply of custard doughnuts and Murphy at my side. He has a knack for smoothing things down, bringing us all together, making us laugh.

'Maybe Brightford Academy wasn't as bad as I thought it would be,' I admit later, walking back to Stella Street Primary. 'It's scary . . . but in a good way. Like a whole new stage of life is opening up for us!'

'Of course it is,' Willow says. 'And hey, the French teacher said she'd never seen such a keen and promising class!'

'I know!' I grin. 'Wait till we come back from Paris – there'll be no stopping us!'

'I'm glad you asked about the classes, Daizy,' Beth says. 'I don't know what I'd do if they split us up. I can survive without lipgloss and eyeliner as long as I have my best mates.'

That makes me smile. Maybe Beth and Willow act all grown-up and confident, but

underneath it all they are the same as always – kind, caring, lovely, loyal.

We turn into the driveway of Stella Street Primary just as the bell for home time peals out, and my world crashes.

Dad's big green van is there, chugging and groaning and belching out clouds of chip-shop smoke as it drives slowly past us. I catch a glimpse of reddish-orange fur behind the wheel, and I feel my cheeks burning.

‘Did that giant red squirrel just wave at you, Daizy?’ Ethan Miller asks.

I think I might die of shame.

Nightmare. It looks like Dad, intrigued by my tales of lentil stew and kidney-bean custard, actually did phone the school and offer to come in to talk to the children about healthy eating. And Stella Street Primary was foolish enough to accept his invitation – thank goodness it was while we were on our taster trip to Brightford Academy.

Pixie, of course, has not been as lucky. She runs towards me across the playground, traumatized, eyes wide, pigtails flying.

'There was this big red squirrel telling us about dandelion leaves and organic bread,' I overhear one of her classmates say to his mum.

'He danced around and sang a song and gave us carob brownies that tasted like dirt. It was scary . . .'

I look at Pixie and she looks at me, her cheeks scarlet. She does not need to tell me out loud that the identity of the giant squirrel must remain a secret. I'd cut my own tongue out rather than tell anyone.

Then I catch sight of Murphy's puzzled face, and realize that he is probably putting two and two together. He lives just along the road from us and, let's face it, he'd have to be blind not to have spotted Dad cycling to work in his squirrel suit this past week, or recognized the van just now. My dark secret is out.

'Murphy?' I ask, as we walk home through the park with Pixie skipping on ahead. 'You know we said a while ago that we'd never keep secrets from each other?'

'Er . . . yes?' Murphy says, looking slightly uncomfortable.

'Remember I told you Dad had a new job?'

'Yes?'

I take a deep breath. 'Well . . . that was him in the squirrel suit just now. He's working for the Squirrel & Lentil Wholefood Café and he's got this dreadful idea of going into schools and preaching to the kids about lentils and beansprouts and nettle soup. It is the most embarrassing thing that has ever happened to me. I mean, my life is over – my dad is a giant red squirrel. It seriously can't get any worse.'

'Right,' Murphy says gently. 'Yeah – I thought that was him . . . It could be worse, Daizy, he could have been dressed as a lentil instead of a squirrel.'

I swallow, hard.

'It's no joke,' I sigh. 'Worrying about Dad's job is the last thing I need just now. I'm kind of worried about starting at Brightford Academy. What if I can't handle it? What if you, me,

Beth and Willow drift apart?'

'Hmmm,' Murphy sighs. 'Actually . . .'

'Actually, it happens a lot,' I frown. 'We have to stick together, Murphy. Friends forever and all that. I have a squirrel for a dad, so Brightford Academy can't scare me, right?'

Murphy looks awkward. 'About that, Daizy . . . there's something I've been meaning to tell you.'

'What?' I quip. 'Don't tell me. Your dad is actually a natterjack toad. Or a wild boar?'

'I'm trying to be serious, Daizy.'

I blink. Serious? I don't like the sound of that.

'OK,' I shrug. 'What's up?'

Murphy looks shifty. 'It's about Brightford Academy,' he begins. 'There's no easy way to say this, Daizy . . .'

I feel cold all over, as if something bad is about to happen. A minute ago I said that things couldn't get any worse, but suddenly I have a strong feeling that actually, maybe they could.

I start to talk, as if an avalanche of words can

stop whatever it is Murphy is trying to tell me.

'I thought it was OK, actually,' I blurt. 'Brightford Academy. Better than I imagined. I am so glad we'll all be in a class together because I couldn't stand it if they split us up. We're friends forever, aren't we – me, you, Beth and Willow? Nothing can ever change that –'

'Daizy,' Murphy interrupts. 'Can you listen for a minute? It's just – well – I might not actually be going to Brightford Academy.'

'What do you mean?' I ask in a small, shocked voice. 'Where else would you go?'

Murphy bites his lip.

'My cousins go to this specialist arts school near Moonleigh,' he tells me. 'Mum thought it would be perfect for me, so we went to look at it a couple of months ago. It's really cool and creative, Daizy, and the facilities are awesome. I had to show them some of my artwork. It's a private school, but they've

offered me a scholarship – they'll pay the fees for me. They think I have real potential.'

A huge lump forms in my throat, as if I have just tried to swallow a tennis ball. I want to speak, but the words are stuck inside me and won't come out. Brightford Academy is scary enough, but Brightford Academy without Murphy? It doesn't bear thinking about. The bottom falls out of my world. I sink down on to a nearby park bench, and Murphy perches beside me. In the distance, I can see Pixie on the

swings, swooping back and forth without a care in the world.

'I should have told you,' he says. 'I know we had a pact not to keep secrets, but I couldn't tell you this . . . I just didn't know how.'

I nod and smile and try to dredge up the words to say I am pleased, proud of him even, but nothing comes out. I should be happy that my talented friend has been given a chance like this. Design is definitely Murphy's star quality, and in a school like that he will get his chance

to shine – but all I can think about is how much I'll miss him.

'It's not boarding school or anything,' Murphy is saying. 'I can take the train every day. We'll still see each other – nothing will change!'

But everything is changing, I know. Friends go to different schools, make new mates. They drift slowly apart until they have nothing at all in common. A year from now, Murphy may just be a boy I used to know, a boy in a fancy blazer who smiles politely when he sees me pass by.

'Say something, Daizy,' Murphy prompts.

My mouth feels like it is full of dust, but I try to be brave.

'It's great, Murphy,' I say, as brightly as I can. 'I am so proud of you. I've always said you were brilliant at all that art and design stuff, and this just proves it. What an opportunity. Cool, totally.'

'Daizy –'

I glance at my wrist, as if checking out a watch I don't have.

'Oh my – is that the time?' I exclaim. 'Pixie!

Pixie, come on! We really have to dash. It's dandelion quiche for tea . . .'

'Hang on,' Murphy says. 'Daizy, don't go –'

But I am already running across the park, yelling for Pixie, my eyes blurred with tears.

7

Murphy tells Beth and Willow about his scholarship place a few days later, and they squeal and whoop and tell him they are pleased for him. They seem to take it all in their stride.

'You can introduce us to all the cool boys at your new school,' Willow tells him. 'Brilliant!'

'Too right,' Beth chimes in. 'Can't wait!'

I wonder if I will ever be cool and grown-up enough not to feel like my heart is breaking at the thought of losing one of my best mates? I doubt it.

Murphy is not going to be the

glue that holds my friendship with Beth and Willow together. He won't even be in the same school. My friendship group is falling to pieces and there's nothing at all I can do about it.

'Cheer up, Daizy,' Murphy says. 'It's not like it's happening yet. It's not even definite, really. Mum said it was up to me to decide. I think she wants me to, though.'

'Won't you miss us?' I ask sadly.

'Of course I will!' he says. 'But you won't be getting rid of me that easily, Daizy Star. You'll still see me all the time – I only live along the road, remember?'

'I know, but –'

'But nothing,' Murphy says firmly. 'It'll all work out, you'll see. And in the meantime, we'll have the Paris trip – the four of us together. It's going to be awesome!'

I guess that's true, at least. The Paris trip could be my last real chance to hang out properly with my friends. Looks like I'd better make the most of it.

Menu

fish & chips
tuna pasta
macaroni cheese
egg salad
nettle flapjack
beansprout soup

At school, Dad's healthy-eating talk has resulted in some horrific additions to the lunch-time menu, including nettle flapjacks and beansprout soup. This is not good.

With the French trip creeping ever closer, I ask the cook to put French Onion Soup and Tarte Tatin on the menu instead, but she just snorts in a very rude way and asks whether I want Toad in the Hole or not. I shake my head, even though I am pretty sure there are no actual toads in it.

'The French eat frogs and snails, you know,' Ethan Miller says helpfully, appearing at my shoulder. 'Toad in the Hole would be just their style.'

'It's just sausages and Yorkshire pudding,' I tell him briskly. 'No toads are involved. And I am not having that, anyhow, because these days I am practically vegan. I do not eat anything that comes from an animal.'

'You'll starve to death in France then,' Ethan smirks.

'I will just eat chocolate croissants,' I shrug, and hope that Ethan doesn't realize that they're not actually vegan either. Luckily, he is too obsessed with football and hair gel to focus on such details.

'This trip is going to be fun,' Ethan says, helping himself to mash and gravy. 'I'm sure we can shake off Miss Moon and the others and have a few adventures on our own. What d'you say, Daizy Star? I'll buy you a chocolate croissant and we can walk along the banks of the River Seine in the moonlight!'

My jaw drops in horror. Escape from Miss Moon and the others? Walk through Paris in the moonlight with Ethan Miller? Is he mad? I would

rather eat one of Dad's nettle flapjacks and wash it down with dandelion squash, and that is NOT happening, trust me.

'No, thank you,' I say primly. 'I do not want to have adventures with you, Ethan Miller. And I can buy my own chocolate croissants, thank you very much!'

'I'm joking, Daizy!' he grins. 'Didn't think I was serious, did you?'

Two little spots of colour appear in my cheeks. I grab a plate of quiche and salad and storm away before they flood my face with a tide of crimson. I cannot stand that boy, really I can't.

I flop down at a table with Willow and Beth, scowling.

'What's up?' Beth asks. 'Ethan Miller been getting on your nerves again?'

'Does he ever do anything else?' I huff.

I swear, if I only had one nerve left in my whole entire body, Ethan Miller would find it and manage to get on it.

'Are you sure we are talking about the same person?' Willow asks. 'He's so cute!'

I decide not to answer. Beth and Willow are hopeless when it comes to Ethan Miller, its' a lost cause.

'He's gorgeous,' Beth sighs, starry-eyed. 'And we are going to be in Paris with him. The city of romance. Anything could happen!'

I pull a face. 'Ethan Miller doesn't have a romantic bone in his body,' I huff. 'I worry about you two sometimes, seriously!'

'Well, don't,' Willow says. 'I happen to think he's cool, OK? And if it took a little bit of Parisian romance to get the two of us together . . . well, what could be wrong with that?'

'Nothing,' Beth says. 'Except that he will fall for me, not you, Willow. I have been in love

with him for years now. So, if there is any romance in the air –'

'Hey, you two,' I cut in. 'Don't fall out over a boy! Especially not Ethan Miller. He is so not worth it!'

'He so IS,' Beth argues. 'But we won't fall out about it, Daizy, don't worry. Willow and I have talked this through. If Ethan decides he likes me best, then Willow will be totally fine with it; if he decides he likes Willow best, then I will try to be happy for her.'

I wonder if I should tell them what Ethan just said to me, but decide against it. He may have been joking, but I am not sure my friends would see the funny side. I definitely didn't.

'All's fair in love and war,' Willow shrugs. 'May the best girl win!'

'Exactly,' Beth agrees. 'And romance is in the air, I'm certain of it. Paris . . . I am counting down the days. I have sneaked some make-up into my suitcase, and Mum says I can buy some new clothes specially. I want

to make sure I look my best in Paris.'

'Me too,' Willow says. 'Maybe the three of us should go shopping together?'

I bite my lip. Money is still ultra-tight at home, even now that Dad is working. I won't be going shopping with Beth and Willow, I know – there is no cash to spare. Besides, their fashion taste just lately is scarily grown-up.

'French girls are very chic,' Beth muses. 'We definitely need new clothes. We don't want to look like schoolkids!'

'We are schoolkids,' I point out, but my friends just laugh.

'I know, but we're practically at secondary school,' Beth grins. 'And we are going on a trip with the cutest boy ever . . . to PARIS! It's a dream come true!'

More of a nightmare if Ethan Miller is involved, I think darkly, but Beth and Willow are miles away now, fantasizing about Paris.

'Sunset over the Seine,' Willow is saying. 'Starry nights above Sacré-Coeur. French

kissing under the Eiffel Tower . . .'

'Willow!' I gasp, shocked. 'There won't be any kissing under the Eiffel Tower, especially not the French sort. Yuk!'

My best friends smile and look at me in a slightly pitying way, as if I am five years old and way too young to understand. Actually, I understand a whole lot more than they know. I am not crushing on Ethan Miller, and that means I can see things a little more clearly. The only person he is in love with is himself, and I don't think any amount of Parisian romance will change that.

My daydreams of hanging out in cool French cafés and sharing fun, freedom and heart-to-hearts with my very best friends are fading fast. When it comes to the Paris trip, it sounds like Beth and Willow have very different plans . . .

8

Miss Moon has our group passport all ready. We have practised our French until it is *très, très bon*, plotted our journey on a big wall map and had a family meeting in the school hall to go over all the details.

Finally, it is actually happening.

'Tomorrow is the big day,' Miss Moon announces. 'I will see you all in the playground at eight o'clock sharp. Set those alarm clocks and be on time – the coach won't wait! *Au revoir, mes enfants!*'

'*Au revoir, Mademoiselle!*' we chorus, and when the bell goes we stampede out of there as if our lives depend on it. I want to get home so I can

check through my suitcase again. I have been packed for approximately seventeen days now, but I want to make sure my clothes for tomorrow are ironed and ready, and that Mum remembered to get secret supplies of non-vegan custard doughnuts for the journey.

When I have checked everything over for the final time, I will have my tea and go to bed early because the sooner morning comes round the better.

Things do not go according to plan.

'Surprise!' Mum says, when Pixie and I get home from school. 'You're off to France in the morning, so your dad suggested a special treat, a meal out to wish you *bon voyage*. What do you think?'

'Cool!' I grin. 'Pizza? With extra cheese and pineapple and hot chocolate fudge cake and ice cream for afters?'

Mum looks shifty. 'Not exactly . . .'

'Fish and chips?' I appeal. 'Ice-cream sundaes?'

Behind Mum, Becca rolls her eyes. 'Bean stew and tofu cake, more like,' she sighs. 'We are going to the Squirrel & Lentil. Dad has reserved a table for us.'

The smile slides from my face.

'Do you want to invite Beth and Willow along?' Mum asks. 'Or Murphy?'

'No!' I say, alarmed. 'They'll be much too busy. Besides . . . it's meant to be a special family meal, right?'

'It's whatever you want it to be,' Mum says.

'Let's make it just us then,' I say guiltily. 'That's what I'd like.'

It is not what I'd like, exactly, but it's a million times better than subjecting my friends to a meal of stewed turnip and alfalfa sprouts. And there is

just NO WAY in the world I will ever live it down if Beth or Willow catch sight of Dad in his giant squirrel suit.

The Squirrel & Lentil doesn't look as bad as I had feared. The tables are draped with red-and-white-checked tablecloths, the walls are painted a cheery yellow and there are some fairly normal people scattered about the place, as well as a few ageing hippies dressed in hand-woven hessian and tasselled velvet flares.

Then I spot Dad, in his squirrel disguise. I paste a frozen smile on my face as he hands us each a menu.

'What do you think?' Dad asks, his fluffy tail bobbing dangerously. 'This café is cool, isn't it? A great place to hang out and drink a banana smoothie or a soya latte. Now you've seen it, you can tell your friends, maybe call in with them now and again after school.'

'Erm . . .' I say awkwardly.

'Well . . .' Pixie cringes.

'Over my dead body,' Becca snaps. My big

sister can be a little blunt at times, but at least she is honest, I guess . . .

'Let's just enjoy our meal, shall we?' Mum sighs. 'This is Daizy's *bon voyage* dinner, so forget the sales pitch. What should we order?'

We finally settle for tofu burgers with rhubarb crumble and soya custard for afters. The burger is OK, especially when smothered in lots of wholefood tomato sauce, but the rhubarb crumble tastes like sour string and grit served up with yellow wallpaper paste. My face is scrunched up with despair after just one bite, and Dad bustles off to the kitchen for date syrup to sweeten the taste before Pixie's cries of disgust upset the other diners.

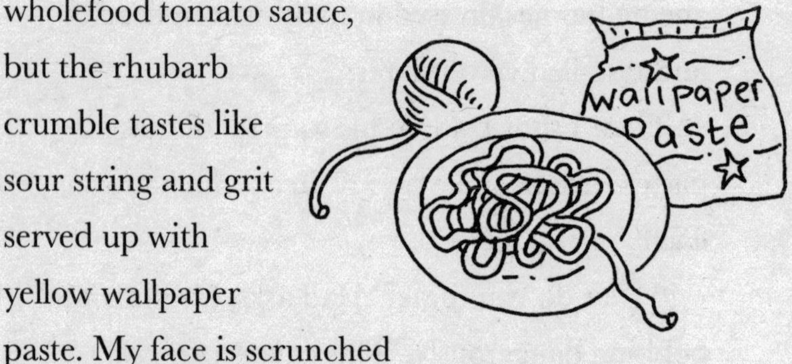

And that is when Ethan Miller walks into the café, carrying a cardboard box of raggedy green leaves.

'Your delivery of farm-fresh wild salad,' he says cheerily to the girl behind the counter, and she takes the box and hands him a tenner from the till.

I panic. Ethan Miller must not see me here. He is the most annoying boy in the whole of Stella Street Primary, and he could never, ever be trusted with the secret of the giant red squirrel. I slide off my chair and try to hide under the table behind the red-checked tablecloth before Ethan has a chance to turn round.

'Daizy?' Mum says, alarmed. 'What are you doing? Are you all right?'

'I dropped my spoon,' I whisper. 'I won't be a minute.'

I cross my fingers and hope that Ethan

vanishes as quickly as he appeared. Why would anyone want to hang around in the Squirrel & Lentil, after all?

Luck is not on my side.

'Hello, Ethan!' Pixie pipes up. 'What are you doing here? Whatever you do, don't buy the rhubarb crumble because my dad invented it and it tastes absolutely revolting.'

Ethan laughs, and as I peer out from under the red-checked tablecloth, I see his feet in muddy trainers approaching the table.

'I'm not eating here,' he says brightly. 'I'm just making a delivery for my uncle. He's a goat farmer, as you know, but lately he has been doing a nice sideline in dandelion and sorrel leaves for the Squirrel & Lentil. They're just weeds, but my uncle says, if people are silly enough to pay good money for them . . .'

'I expect they are very tasty weeds,' Mum says politely.

'Is this a family outing then?' Ethan asks. 'Where's Daizy?'

My heart sinks.

'Under the table, looking for a spoon,' Pixie chirps, and the next thing I know the red-checked tablecloth is lifted up and Ethan's grinning face appears.

'Daizy,' he says. 'Why am I not surprised?'

'Ethan,' I growl. 'Fancy seeing you here.' I crawl out from my hiding place, a little red-faced, while Mum asks Ethan if he is looking forward to the Paris trip.

'Definitely,' he says. 'We can't wait, can we, Daizy? Paris in the spring . . . ooh la la!'

My face turns purple with rage, then drains of colour completely as Dad appears from the kitchen in his squirrel finery, brandishing the date syrup. 'Here we are!' he calls over. 'A little swirl of this will soon put the smiles back on your faces!'

Ethan smirks. 'Bizarre place, this,' he says. 'I'm not sure about the squirrel guy, are you?'

'We have never been sure about the squirrel guy,' Becca says with a sigh, but Mum just laughs.

'Ethan . . . this is Daizy's dad,' she announces. 'Mike, this is Daizy's schoolfriend, Ethan. His uncle supplies your wild salad leaves, isn't that amazing?'

'Amazing!' Dad beams, his tufty ears twitching

and his tail swaying slightly. 'Nice to meet you, Ethan!'

He shakes hands with Ethan and I close my eyes and cover my ears so I do not have to see Ethan's grin or hear his snorting laugh. It is too, too shameful.

When I open my eyes again, Ethan is on his way out, waving and winking at me in a way that leaves me certain he will make my life a misery from now on with his squirrelly little secret.

9

The next morning, I am up before dawn and dressed soon after in an outfit I bought last weekend from a charity shop in town. I look cool, calm and very, very French in my stripy top, dark shades and black beret – exactly like the cartoon pictures in Miss Moon's *French For Beginners* book.

'Is this a joke?' Becca asks over the breakfast table. 'Daizy, you cannot

go to France looking like that! People will laugh!'

I tilt my chin in the air. Becca may be the best big sister in the world but she is wrong about this. I am French at heart, I'm certain of it, and I just want to look the part.

An hour later, I'm feeling less certain. Beth and Willow laughed when they saw my beret, shades and stripy top, and asked me where I'd left my garlic and my baguette. I explained that I would be adding those accessories once I actually got to France, but they just giggled and rolled their eyes, which was not encouraging.

I thought friends were supposed to be supportive? If Beth and Willow are being this weird about shades, a beret and a stripy top, they definitely cannot find out about Dad's giant squirrel suit. I'd never hear the last of it. If word got out it would destroy any hope of me settling in well at Brightford Academy. I'd be a laughing stock.

Still, my secret should be safe in Paris – as long as I can bribe Ethan Miller into silence.

'Does wandering about in fancy dress run in your family?' he asks brightly, as we climb the steps up into the coach.

'Do not mention the giant red squirrel,' I hiss under my breath.

'What's it worth to stay silent?' Ethan grins, winking horribly.

I grit my teeth and slip him one of my emergency custard doughnuts. It shuts him up – for now at least. I have a feeling I haven't heard the last of it, though.

'Do I look like I'm in fancy dress?' I appeal to Murphy, as we settle into our seats.

'No-o, not exactly,' he sighs kindly. 'You are just pushing back the barriers, making a style statement. If you can't do that in Paris, then where can you? Paris is the fashion capital of the world!'

'Exactly,' I say. 'I'll fit in perfectly once I get there, right?'

Murphy looks uncertain. 'Maybe,' he says.

Miss Moon checks the register one last time and the coach revs and purrs into life. Mum, Dad, Becca and Pixie wave from the playground with all the other families as we move off across the car park and out into the road.

I feel a stab of sadness as I wave back. Even though Dad has the most embarrassing job in the world, I love him, especially when he is not wearing his dodgy squirrel suit. Mum is the best mum in the universe, and Becca and Pixie are without a doubt the coolest sisters ever. I adjust my dark shades bravely.

A lot is riding on this trip. It may not have started well, but I know I can turn that around. I need to reconnect with my best friends and find a way to keep us close; and, of course, I must discover my destiny. The final quest for my star quality has begun!

I stagger off the coach that afternoon, crumpled, tired and slightly travel-sick after a choppy ferry

crossing and hours on a French Autoroute. It is a long way from Brightford to Paris, but we are here now, and I can't stop smiling.

We pick up our bags and follow Miss Moon to the Hotel Escargot, a small, budget hotel tucked away above a café. The sun is shining and people are sitting at pavement tables, reading French newspapers and sipping café au lait, while a skinny, scruffy white cat slinks along beneath the tables, looking for scraps. It all looks so cool . . . so French!

'Wow!' Beth whispers. 'I can't believe it! We are in Paris!'

'At last,' Willow breathes.

'*Très, très froid*,' I agree.

Some of the French people give me funny looks as I follow my friends into the café. I expect this is because I do not look like a British schoolgirl but an actual French girl. I smile sweetly from behind my shades, then bump into one of the café tables. Ethan Miller laughs and tells me I'll probably break my neck if I insist on wearing sunglasses inside, which totally shows how little he knows about being French.

A plump, smiley woman called Madame Le Chapeau welcomes us in heavily accented English.

'*Bonjour, bonjour*,'

she says, grinning. 'You are all most welcome to the Hotel Escargot and to Paris! Please be at home and enjoy it all . . . let me know if there is anything you need! This is my father, Pierre . . . he will show you to your rooms, *tout de suite*!'

An elderly man with a big white moustache, a blue waistcoat and a real, genuine French beret ambles towards us. I elbow Beth and Willow. 'See!' I whisper. 'They do wear berets! I told you!'

Pierre picks up a couple of suitcases and leads the way up the winding staircase. The girls are on the first floor, our rooms ranged along the hallway, each with several beds and a shared bathroom. I am sharing with Beth and Willow. Miss Moon and Miss Kelly, the

teaching assistant, have a room at the end of the hall, and the boys are on the top floor with Mr March, the football coach, who has been roped in as an extra helper.

'You will be comfortable, I hope,' Pierre says. 'Just call me if there is anything you need, *oui*? I am happy to help!'

Pierre has the same strong accent as Madame Le Chapeau. He says 'zee' instead of 'the' and 'zer' instead of 'there'. It is just too exciting for words. We are actually here, in Paris, in FRANCE, with real, live French people!

If I peer over the edge of the top bunk and squint through the blossom on the trees outside the window, I can actually see the Eiffel Tower in the distance. Beth says it is just a very tall electricity pylon, but I disagree. I wish I had thought of bringing binoculars or a telescope, for proof.

'We are actually 'ere,' I sigh. 'In zee capital city of art and culture and 'istory. Eet ees so exciting!'

My friends stare at me, horrified.

'Why are you talking like that?' Willow asks.

'Everybody talks like zis, 'ere,' I shrug.

Willow puts her hands on her hips. 'That is because they are French people, trying to speak English,' she says sternly. 'You actually ARE English, Daizy, so why are you speaking with a funny French accent? They'll think you are making fun of them!'

I blink. 'I'm not!' I protest, reverting back to my usual accent at once. 'It's because I admire them! I want to be just like them!'

'Is that what the stripy T-shirt and the beret and the shades are all about?' Beth asks. 'Are you trying to look French? I thought it was some kind of joke!'

'It's not a joke!' I say in a small voice. 'I feel French. Maybe it's my star quality!'

'Daizy,' Beth says patiently. 'Being French is NOT a star quality. It's just something you are . . . or not. And you are not!'

'Inside I am!' I say stubbornly.

'You were born in Brightford!' Willow points out. 'So were your parents, and theirs. You're not French!'

My shoulders droop. 'I'd like to be,' I sigh. In my imagination, the French are everything I want to be: cool, sophisticated, mysterious . . . and a safe distance from the dangers of giant red squirrels. But the truth is I am not French, and I never will be.

'A star quality is different,' Beth says. 'It's about skill, talent. It could be ballet, like me, or singing, like Willow, or football, like Ethan, or art, like Murphy Malone. You just haven't found yours yet.'

'I know,' I say sadly. 'But I am close. I can sense it, feel it. I will find my star quality in France, I know it!'

'Relax about the star quality thing,' Willow says, a little irritated. 'It's getting to be a bit of an obsession.'

'What do you mean?'

'Sometimes it's like it's all you ever think

about,' Beth sighs. 'All this year. Seriously, Daizy. Forget the star quality. Just be yourself!'

Hurt stings me, sharp as a slap. Obsessed? The injustice of it curls around my heart. Why can't Beth and Willow understand? After all, they each have a star quality and I don't. As for 'being myself' – well, who else would I be?

They drift back to the bathroom to get changed and I am left alone, wondering if the only thing I can actually feel in the air is cheap bodyspray and the faint aroma of coffee wafting up from downstairs.

It is not enough to look the part, to speak fluent French or eat croissants every day. If 'being French' is not my hidden talent, well, I will just have to work out what is . . .

10

The next morning we are up early, eating croissants and sipping hot chocolate in the Hotel Escargot café. Pierre is sitting in the corner, drawing in a big sketchbook, and I sneak over to look. He has drawn a portrait of Ethan Miller eating a croissant, and it is awesome.

'Wow!' I breathe. 'Pierre, you are a real, live artist!'

'It's a hobby of mine,' he shrugs. 'Since I've retired. It's my dream – sometimes I go up to Sacré-Coeur and sketch for

the tourists, but mostly I'm happy to draw here. I have a little studio, a shed in the yard. I will show you perhaps, while you are here.'

'Please!' I say. 'That would be cool. We are going to some art galleries today, and tomorrow we're doing some drawings of our own.'

Pierre smiles. 'All the best artists have lived and worked in Paris. It's a very inspiring city!'

'I think so too,' I say. I am wondering if perhaps art might be my star quality, and if Pierre could give me a few tips, when Miss Moon calls me over to join the others. We set off to the Louvre, one of the most famous museums in the world. The little white cat I saw last night follows us all the way to the Métro station.

'D'you think that cat is OK?' I ask Beth and

Willow. 'It looks a bit lost . . .'

But when I look round, the cat has vanished, and Miss Moon ushers us down into the Métro.

At the Louvre we take a tour of the most famous paintings, which are very old and very serious. I cannot help noticing that some of the people in those pictures have forgotten to put their clothes on, and Ethan Miller notices too and snorts with laughter and says 'ooh la la!' over and over until Miss Moon tells him to get a grip.

'Got any more secret custard doughnuts SQUIRRELLED away, Daizy?' Ethan asks later, smirking, as I sit outside the Louvre in the sunshine eating my packed lunch.

'Shhh!' I hiss, furious. 'You said you wouldn't mention squirrels!'

'Did I? I don't remember that . . .'

I fish another smuggled doughnut out of my bag and hand it over. 'No more squirrel jokes, Ethan,' I scowl. 'Deal?'

'Probably,' he says. 'Maybe. But . . . what if I forget?'

'Don't,' I hiss. 'Or I'll have to find a way of shutting you up!'

'Promises, promises,' Ethan laughs, and saunters away with doughnut crumbs all over his face.

We pile on to the Métro to go to our next art gallery, the Centre Pompidou. Murphy sits beside me, his eyes bright.

'Having fun, Daizy?' he wants to know.

'Paris is amazing,' I sigh. 'I could stay here forever! Or . . . well, until the end of the trip, anyway.'

'I know,' Murphy grins. 'Did you like the Louvre? Cool, huh?'

'Sure,' I agree, although I am actually not very sure at all. 'It's just that those pictures

were all so . . . grand. And serious.'

Murphy frowns. 'Maybe the Louvre wasn't quite your style. Wait till you see the stuff at the Centre Pompidou – I've been researching it. People don't always understand modern art, but it's cutting-edge stuff, worth millions. It'll blow your socks off, Daizy!'

I raise an eyebrow. My socks are over-the-knee ones, red with little black spots and tassels dangling from the top. I am not sure anything could blow them off, especially art, but you never know.

The Centre Pompidou is huge, all plate glass and shiny surfaces, with a giant escalator inside a glass tube, like those weird tunnels you get in a hamster cage. Inside it's even weirder.

'This is modern art at its best,' Miss Moon tells us. 'Look around, see what you make of it.

I'll meet you back at the escalators at four o'clock. Perhaps it will inspire you for tomorrow's sketching trip! Off you go!'

Beth, Willow and Murphy drag me off through the big, airy gallery. 'Wow,' Murphy says, as we pause in front of a huge canvas splattered with a rainbow of sludge-thick paint. 'I mean . . . wow!'

'It's a mess,' Beth huffs.

'My little brother could do better,' Willow says. 'And he's only three. What do you think, Daizy?'

I think that this modern art stuff is a waste of time. You might as well throw your dinner at the wall, and there was a portrait in one of the galleries where the woman had two noses, three eyes and skin the colour of a mouldy lemon.

I remember what Murphy said earlier about

it being cutting-edge stuff and hard to understand and worth a fortune. People actually pay millions for this stuff? I reckon I could do better, even wearing a blindfold.

'Unbelievable,' I say. 'Incredible. Astonishing.'

And it is. These paintings are chaotic, crazy, toe-curlingly weird. They look like the aftermath of a hurricane, or our kitchen when Pixie has been baking neon cupcakes. I start to smile. How hard can it be?

Maybe I have just found my hidden talent after all.

Later, back at the Hotel Escargot, Pierre takes Beth, Willow, Murphy and me on a guided tour of his studio, a big, airy shed behind the main hotel building. I spot the little white cat slinking along the wall, but when I nudge Murphy to point it out, the cat melts away into the shadows.

There are windows all along one side of the studio shed, and the table is crammed with jars, brushes, palettes and paint. In one corner there

seed
oil

is an old comfy chair and an easel, with finished paintings leaning against the studio walls.

'It's perfect,' I tell Pierre.

'It's my hideaway,' Pierre shrugs. 'The place I am truly happy.'

Perhaps, if I were an artist, I could be truly happy too?

We spend the evening watching a jazz band play in the café. Jazz is not my favourite kind of music. I am more of a thrash-punk-metal kind of girl – I even had a band with Beth, Willow and Murphy, once. Still, there is something very cool and romantic about watching people play saxophone and trumpet in a candlelit Parisian café.

I sit beside Pierre, who is sketching the musicians. 'Can anybody be an artist, do you think?' I ask him.

'It's a gift,' Pierre tells me. 'Anyone can try, yes, but true art comes from the soul!'

I nod wisely. I have art in my soul too – it has probably been there all along, without me even

knowing. I watch Pierre sketch the figures, then mix up watercolour paint to swish over the images. Colour blurs and blossoms, and the painting comes to life. I am learning more by watching Pierre than from a million art lessons at school, pushing poster paint around on grey, cardboardy paper.

'I think I might be an artist too,' I tell Pierre. 'Miss Moon is taking us sketching tomorrow – do you want to come too?'

'Tomorrow? *Non, ma petite Daizy,* I will be at Place du Tertre, in the artists' quarter. A famous gallery owner is coming to look for new talent for an exhibition. It's an opportunity I cannot miss!'

'A famous gallery owner?' I echo. 'An exhibition?'

I hope that Pierre's work is spotted and chosen for the exhibition, but maybe more than one new talent could be discovered?

A plan begins to form in my mind. If I can make sure Miss Moon takes us to the Place du Tertre on our sketching tour, the gallery owner

might spot my unique style. I could shoot to fame overnight!

The jazz band is still playing down in the café as we switch out the lights and snuggle down into bed. My star quality is so close now that I could reach out and touch it.

'Today has been the best day of my entire life,' I whisper into the darkness. 'The day I discovered who I really am . . .'

'You are Daizy Star,' Willow informs me sleepily. 'Age eleven, of 17 Silver Street, Brightford.'

'I know that,' I sigh.

What Willow doesn't understand is that my days in Brightford are numbered. I belong here, in Paris, painting pictures on the banks of the River Seine and being rich and famous. People will flock from miles around to admire my paintings; schoolchildren will study my creations. Beth and Willow will be sorry they doubted me then.

'I've had a vision,' I say bravely. 'A glimpse

of the future . . .' I take a deep breath. Why keep it secret? My friends will find out sooner or later, and if I don't share it soon I might just explode.

'I am going to be a famous artist!' I blurt out.

But there is no response at all, just the sound of steady breathing in the dark room. They've fallen asleep.

Over breakfast (brioche and cheese today) Miss Moon runs through the day's schedule. We are going to the church of Sacré-Coeur, then sketching outside before heading back to the hotel for lunch.

My hand shoots up.

'Miss?' I ask. 'Can we do our sketching in the Place du Tertre, like the real artists? Pierre will be there today – he could show us what to do. It would be *très, très froid*!'

'Yes, Pierre was telling me about that,' Miss Moon says. 'I don't see why we shouldn't go – we're passing by anyway, and it might be fun to be part of the hustle and bustle for a little while.

As long as you all have one good drawing by the end of the morning, that's fine.'

We follow Miss Moon through the narrow streets leading up to Sacré-Coeur, clipboards and paper tucked under our arms. I glance behind me once or twice, and each time I spot the scrawny white cat darting in and out of doorways. Is it following me?

It's quite breezy, and my hair whips around my face as we walk. We climb the steps up to the beautiful old church with its white domes and pillars, and Miss Moon leads us inside. It's cool and quiet and peaceful, with a golden mosaic picture stretching across the domed ceiling and stained-glass windows that spill jewel-bright colours across the church. We spread out and start to draw, but my sketches look like a three-year-old might have done them. This is a very good thing when it comes to modern art, of course, but not so good when Ethan Miller is peering over your shoulder, snorting with laughter.

I put my clipboard away.

I spot a nun, serene in her plain black dress and angled headdress, praying under a statue of a saint. She lights a candle that flickers in the half-light on the little stepped altar beneath the statue.

Miss Moon sees me looking and explains. 'It's a tradition,' she says. 'You buy the candle, say a prayer and light it.'

'Like making a wish?'

'A little,' Miss Moon smiles. 'With a prayer, you have God on your side too. Would you like to try?'

We all spend our change on candles. Beth says a prayer for her gran; Willow says one for world peace; I say one for future success as a famous artist. Beth and Willow exchange glances, then laugh so hard they have to hide behind their hands to calm down again.

'Good one, Daizy,' Beth says. 'You really had me there!'

'I know,' Willow smirks. 'For a minute, I

thought you actually meant it!'

'I did,' I say coldly, and they laugh even harder. Even Murphy can't quite meet my eye, and he is totally my artiest mate, so you'd think he might understand. This is not the kind of support I was hoping for. I am still staring at the flickering candle flames when someone sneaks up behind me.

'Dear Lord, keep us safe from giant red squirrels,' Ethan Miller sniggers, and I jab him hard with my elbow.

Outside, the sun is shining as we walk a few streets along to Place du Tertre. It is the most amazing place I have ever seen. The square is edged with cafés, dotted with trees and stuffed with artists making sketches, paintings and caricatures. There are easels and paint palettes, huge canvasses and little sketchbooks, even artists making clay sculptures and random shapes out of wire and plastic.

Tourists wander among them, taking photos, posing for portraits, bartering prices for scary

neon abstract paintings that look like a cross between a pizza and a rubbish dump. I cannot see Pierre in the crowd, and I have no idea if the famous gallery owner is here, but I love the buzz of it all. It's the perfect place for me to take the first step in my career as an artist.

'You've seen a lot of paintings in Paris,' Miss Moon tells us. 'Now it's time to create your own piece of art – look at the trees, the flowers, the shops and houses with their wooden shutters. Look at the artists, or the tourists drinking café au lait . . . this is the heart of creative Paris, children. I want you to be a part of it!'

My heart is racing. My chance to be a real artist at last!

'It's breezy today, so keep your paper clipped firmly to the boards,' Miss Moon instructs. 'Stay in the square, and aim to get one drawing or painting finished. We'll meet back here at midday. Miss Kelly, Mr March and I will keep an eye on you and help if you have any problems!'

She sets down a basket of pastels, paints, brushes and crayons, telling us to choose our materials, and I pick out a little tin of

watercolours, a brush and a plastic beaker which I fill with water. I settle myself on a doorstep with a perfect view of the square.

'Working on a masterpiece, Daizy?' Willow grins, leaning against a nearby tree.

'Good luck, Van Gogh!' Beth teases.

I can't see the funny side, though. Why won't my friends understand? This is my future as a world-famous modern painter they are mocking. I frown, leaning the clipboard against my knees. A cool breeze lifts the corner of the clean, white paper and I smooth it down again sadly.

Lots of famous artists came to Paris in the past, according to Pierre. Were they misunderstood by their friends too? According to Miss Moon, Van Gogh never sold a single painting in his entire lifetime. He got really fed up and cut off his own ear. She showed us a painting of him with his head all bandaged up, which just goes to show that even great artists are not always appreciated.

I do not plan to let things go that far, of course. If I am not rich or famous within the first few weeks, I will give up and move on . . . with both ears intact.

It's worrying, though, that Beth and Willow are acting this way. A few years ago they'd never have teased me. Is this the way things will be at Brightford Academy, without Murphy to keep the peace?

I dip my brush into the water and fill the indents in the lid of the paintbox with pools of liquid red, yellow, blue and green, the way I saw Pierre do last night.

I pick up my pencil and start drawing the tree in front of me. It doesn't look much like a tree, more like a badly mauled cabbage, but I remind myself that modern art does not have to look anything like real life. I sketch in the café across the square. It looks a little lopsided and I have to change the shape to fit it all in. I draw in the shutters and they look like rotten teeth hanging on by a thread, which makes me frown. I draw

one of the tourists and it looks like a stick man with three arms and a blob for a head.

I look anxiously across at Beth and Willow, but Miss Moon is busy showing them how to use charcoal. To my left, Murphy is on his knees on the pavement, making bold sweeps across his paper with bright pastels. His picture will be cool – he's brilliant at drawing.

I am just not sure that I am, and that might be a stumbling block in my quest to become a famous artist. What's the point of having art in your soul if it can't actually get out?

I load my brush with runny green watercolour and touch it to the paper. Green paint drips down across the page. How are you supposed to control it? The wind whips my hair across my face again and I reach up to tuck it behind my ear and manage to dip my elbow in red paint and drag it across my drawing.

Who am I kidding? I am not going to be a famous artist, not ever. I am clumsy and clueless. I will never be spotted by a famous gallery

owner and my pictures will never hang in an exhibition.

It looks like Beth and Willow are right – the whole idea is one big joke.

12

I sigh. There goes yet another failed star quality. My friends are acting all weird on me and there's a sad ache in my chest whenever I remember that Murphy will be going to a different school. Some school trip this is turning out to be.

I notice the scruffy cat again, skulking in a doorway, miaowing loudly. She is a very bedraggled cat, but cute.

'Hello,' I say softly. 'I keep seeing you . . . do you live near here? Or are you a stray? You're very thin . . .'

I reach out a hand to stroke her, and she purrs and arches her back, pressing against my leg. I feed her some leftover cheese from yesterday's packed lunch, and she bolts it down as if she hasn't eaten for days.

'Another star quality bites the dust,' I tell the cat sadly, and she blinks her green eyes as if she actually understands. I'm not sure she does, though – perhaps she is just looking for more cheese? She paws at my bag, sniffing hopefully, then nudges the paint tin with a grubby paw. The palette tips on to my drawing, drenching it with waterfalls of colour.

'Noooo!' I yell, pulling my ruined sketch off the clipboard. 'Shooo! Bad cat!'

The breeze lifts the paper right out of my hands. It lands on the pavement, wet paint running in all directions, and the scruffy cat leaps on it, flicking it up into the air like a new toy.

'Stop!' I squeal, abandoning my clipboard and running to the rescue. The picture may be hopeless, but I have to hand something in to

Miss Moon. I glance over my shoulder to where my teacher is still chatting to Beth and Willow – none of them have noticed my flyaway painting.

I reach out, but the breeze picks up the paper again, whirling it through the air. A tourist steps on it, a bicycle runs over it. The cat and I chase after, dodging among the crowd of tourists. The picture whirls up against an easel painting, picking up a print of sticky oil paint, finally coming to a halt near a little knot of street artists. I spot a familiar face. Black beret, white moustache . . . Pierre is standing at an easel, painting.

'Pierre!' I yell. 'Help! My picture!'

He turns towards me, waving, then spots the tattered paper. Before he can rescue it, a man with a spotty bow tie bends down to pick it off the ground. He begins to talk loudly in streams of rapid French and a crowd of onlookers gather round him as he shows them the picture.

My face floods with crimson. It's bad enough that my star quality has been dashed to pieces before it even began; now I have some weird bloke laughing about it in front of a bunch of French street artists. I elbow my way to the front of the crowd. 'Pierre?' I appeal. 'Can you tell him I want my picture back, please?'

'Wait a moment,' Pierre tells me. 'Jacques, in English, *oui*? So that my friend Daizy can understand?'

Bow-tie Guy looks at me and nods. 'Extraordinary,' he says, squinting at my picture. 'I've never seen anything like it! Look at the colour! Look at the texture! *Zut alors!*'

Up close, I can see that little bits of cut grass, twigs and feathers are stuck to the paint, and a

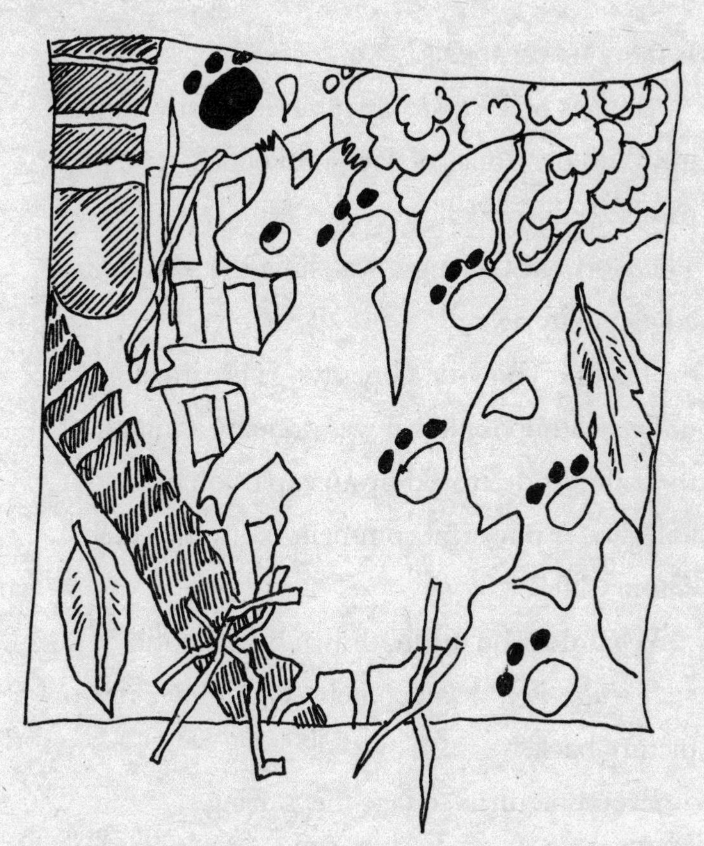

faint trail of rainbow-bright cat prints can be seen moving from right to left. In one corner the tread of a tourist's walking boot is visible, the muddy brown print of the bicycle tyre slicing up through the middle of it. Worst of all, the random blotches of red paint look exactly like a big red squirrel, complete with fluffy tail.

Is there no escape?

'Shades of Picasso,' an American lady chips in. 'With overtones of Jackson Pollock. The paw prints are inspired!'

I snort back a laugh, watching the scruffy cat edge quietly away.

'Unique,' Bow-tie Guy says. 'The drawing underneath looks like it was done by a lunatic, then almost destroyed by an explosion of colour and dirt. A powerful comment on twenty-first-century life!'

What does he mean, drawn by a lunatic?

'*Excusez-moi*,' I say politely. 'Can I have my picture back?'

Everyone turns to face me, staring.

'This is Miss Daizy Star,' Pierre explains. 'She is a British schoolgirl, staying with us at the Hotel Escargot.'

'You . . . YOU are the artist?' Bow-tie Guy asks, wide-eyed. 'But you are just a child!'

'I'm eleven,' I say huffily. 'Practically a teenager!'

Bow-tie Guy isn't even listening. 'How did you do this?' he demands. 'Who is your teacher? This is . . . a work of genius!'

Genius? I stare at the crumpled, paint-stained paper, baffled.

'May I introduce myself?' Bow-tie Guy says. 'I am Jacques Genet, I have a gallery close by. Have you exhibited your work here in Paris?'

I shake my head, still waiting for the punchline of the joke, but it doesn't come. Jacques Genet hands me a gold-edged card with an address printed on it, and it finally dawns on me. He is the gallery owner Pierre was telling me about – and he likes my ruined picture.

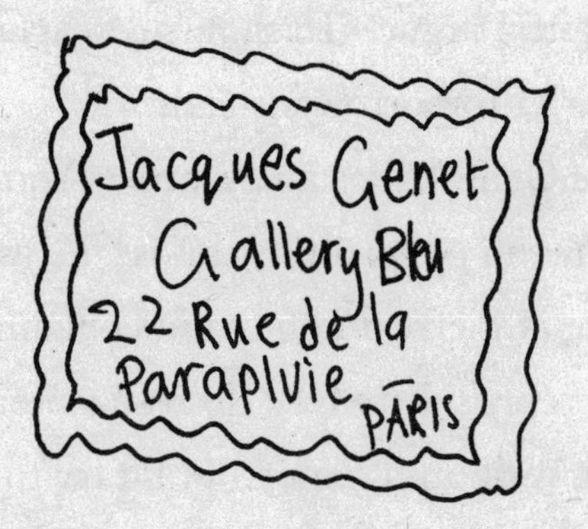

'Do you have more paintings, Daizy Star?' he asks. 'I am putting together an exhibition of new talent. I would very much like to include your work!'

'I don't have any more,' I admit. 'But I could do some!'

'*Fantastique!*' Jacques Genet beams. 'I will just take this . . .' He grips my exploding-squirrel painting, and I panic. According to Jacques, I have just created a masterpiece – even if it was by accident. Surely that's worthy of Miss Moon's famous Star of the Week award? If he takes my painting now, I'll have nothing to show Miss Moon.

'I need it!' I argue. 'To show my teacher! Can I hand it over tomorrow instead?'

Jacques Genet raises an eyebrow. 'You do realize what an opportunity this is?' he asks.

I glance at Pierre and he smiles encouragingly.

'Yes,' I reply solemnly. 'I do realize, really I do. If you can wait until tomorrow, I'll try to do some more paintings too. OK?'

Jacques Genet shakes my hand. 'Very well, I will collect it tomorrow afternoon from the Hotel Escargot. I shall look forward to this. It will be an honour to work with such a promising young artist, Daizy Star!'

I blink, amazed. A promising young artist? Me? Wow!

Sadly, Miss Moon is not quite as impressed.

'Oh dear!' she says, when we spread out our pictures back in the café at the Hotel Escargot. 'What a pity, Daizy! It's ruined!'

My shoulders slump. One minute my picture is a work of genius . . . the next it is back to being a wreck again.

'It's supposed to look like that,' I say stubbornly. 'It is a powerful comment on twenty-first-century life!'

'It looks like a big red squirrel,' Ethan says. 'In an abstract sort of a way, of course. What inspired you, Daizy? Are red squirrels a favourite of yours?'

'Shut up, Ethan!' I howl, outraged.

'Now, now,' Miss Moon sighs. 'Ethan is just trying to be helpful.'

I know better, of course. Ethan Miller does not have a helpful bone in his body. He is trying to stir things up, make me squirm, and he has succeeded. I look to Beth and Willow for support, but that's a mistake too. When will I ever learn?

'Looks like you found it in a rubbish bin,' Willow smirks.

'It's like an explosion in a paint factory,' Beth grins. 'Never mind, Daizy!'

But I do mind. I am outraged. How can my friends be so harsh, so dismissive? I am a promising young artist, a genius of modern painting, and all they can do is mock me.

I can't wait until tomorrow, when Jacques Genet turns up to take my picture to the exhibition. My friends will be sorry they laughed and Miss Moon will realize that she has had a genius in her class all along.

I eat my lunch alone by way of protest, but

Beth and Willow are so busy flirting with Ethan Miller they don't even notice. Seriously, with friends like these, who needs enemies?

I am still not talking to Beth and Willow later as we take a boat trip down the Seine, but they don't seem to have actually realized yet, which is deeply annoying. Murphy is clowning around with some of the boys and I am left alone at the back of the boat with my clipboard of sketches. It feels very lonely.

Is this what it will be like at Brightford Academy? Will I be a loner, an outsider, a friend-free zone? Will I drop so far off Beth and Willow's radar that they forget I ever existed? Secondary school is looking grimmer by the minute, and I am not even there yet.

Afterwards, we walk along the Left Bank and eat crêpes at a riverside stall. I focus on my sketching, but even that isn't looking good. I need inspiration, or mud and footprints and oil paint at the very least. I smear a bit of my chocolate crêpe across a sketch of the Seine,

drop it into a puddle and jump up and down on it a few times. It's not easy being a genius of modern art. Actually, it's not even fun. I am not totally sure I've found the right star quality for me, but as there doesn't seem to be a whole lot of choice I am probably stuck with it.

'What are you doing?' Murphy asks, peering over my shoulder.

'Modern art,' I sigh. 'I want to make another painting like the red squirrel one. You know the sort of thing – a powerful comment on twenty-first-century life. Only I can't quite get it to work . . .'

'How did you do it before?'

I bite my lip. 'It was an accident,' I admit. 'A cat spilt paint on my drawing, a bicycle ran over it, the wind blew it right across the square and then a man with a bow tie said it was a work of genius. He's coming to pick it up for an important exhibition tomorrow afternoon, and I need to do some more by then.'

'Ri-ight,' Murphy sighs. 'A work of genius, huh? Looks like you need a cat, a bicycle and a small whirlwind. At least you've got till tomorrow to think of something.'

'I will,' I say. 'This is my star quality, Murphy. I'm an artist – why can't Beth and Willow be happy for me?'

Murphy frowns. 'I think they're worried you're trying too hard,' he says. 'Setting yourself up for

a fall – like when you were going to be a thrash-punk-metal star, or the first pre-teen supermodel. They know how sad you were when those things didn't work out. They don't want you to get hurt, Daizy, that's all.'

'I won't,' I insist. 'This will work out, you'll see! I thought you of all people would understand. You're going to a special arts school, aren't you, so you can be a designer?'

'Maybe,' Murphy shrugs. 'I haven't decided yet. Sometimes, Daizy, friends are more important.'

What does that mean? I used to think friends were the most important things in the world, but now I am not so sure. This Paris trip is not working out the way I had hoped. Instead of bringing Beth, Willow, Murphy and me closer, it seems to be pushing us apart.

Back at the hotel, Madame Le Chapeau makes us hot chocolate and we sit in the café chatting about the day's adventures. At least, I would be chatting if I wasn't feeling so miffed, and if Beth and Willow could tear themselves away from Ethan Miller.

Outside the window, the stray cat dawdles past, gazing in with slanted green eyes. She is probably feeling almost as lonely as I am. It is no fun at all to be lost, alone, unloved.

'There's that poor cat again,' I say, breaking my silence with Beth and Willow. 'Should we try to rescue her, d'you think?'

'I don't see any cat,' Beth says irritably, tearing her eyes away from Ethan for a millisecond.

'It's just a stray,' Willow huffs. 'What were you saying, Ethan?'

I roll my eyes. When Ethan is around, my best friends may as well be on another planet.

Once upon a time, they'd have helped me in my quest to rescue the little stray, but it looks like I'm on my own with this. Am I the only one

around here who actually cares about homeless, starving cats? Looks like it.

'Miss Moon?' I appeal. 'I think that little cat out there is lost. It needs a home. Can we take it back to Brightford with us?'

'Daizy, that wouldn't be allowed,' my teacher says. 'There are very strict rules about taking animals to Britain. I'm sorry.'

I turn to Murphy. 'Maybe we could get the Hotel Escargot to adopt the stray cat?' I appeal. 'That'd be really cool!'

He frowns. 'I don't think so, Daizy,' he says. 'There are loads of health and hygiene regulations for cafés. I don't think cats are allowed. Although Pierre might let it stay in his studio shed . . .'

'Great idea!' I grin. 'You're a hero, Murphy Malone!'

I run across to where Pierre is sketching, and the story of the stray cat tumbles out. 'Please can you give her a home?' I beg. 'She'd be no trouble, a perfect artist's cat. It's all because of her that

I – um – created – my masterpiece of modern art. She spilt the paint on it and then the wind whisked it right across the square . . .'

I stop, realizing I have just confessed that my painting was an accident and not the result of my inner artistic genius, but Pierre doesn't seem to mind.

'Ah,' he nods wisely. 'I did wonder. Don't worry, Jacques Genet need never know – and if he says it is a work of genius, then of course, it is! As for the cat, yes, she can stay in my studio shed. Let's go and find her . . .'

'Thank you, Pierre!' I say.

Half an hour later, the cat has been fed, watered and given a cushion to sleep on. Pierre names her Picasso and says he has always wanted a cat, and that perhaps she will bring him luck.

I am glad for Picasso because she isn't lost or alone any more, but as I watch Beth, Willow and Murphy, playing a board game now as they eat macaroons and sip hot chocolate, I know I feel lonelier than ever. I have found my star quality

here in Paris, but . . . it doesn't feel as good as I thought it would because, somewhere along the way, I seem to have lost my friends . . .

'Today,' Beth sighs, brushing her long fair hair until it gleams, 'today we are going to the Eiffel Tower, the most romantic place in the whole of Paris. And there, finally, Ethan will ask me out.'

Willow smirks. 'Good luck with that,' she says, painting silver sparkles across her cheekbones. 'It's me he likes. He'll most probably ask ME out, Beth, so try not to be too disappointed.'

'It's YOU who will be disappointed,' Beth says snippily.

The alarm went off exactly five minutes ago, and already my friends are scrapping over stupid Ethan Miller. This is the last day of our Paris

trip, our last chance to chill out and have fun, and already it has disaster written all over it. Not only have I fallen out with my best friends, now they're falling out with each other too.

'Stop squabbling,' I huff, pulling on cut-off jeans, my stripy top and beret. 'You can't argue over a boy! It's ridiculous!'

They turn on me.

'You'll understand one day,' Willow says. 'When YOU fall in love!'

'Trust me,' I scowl. 'That is NEVER going to happen.'

Beth and Willow exchange one of those smug, knowing looks that make me want to scream. 'Paris is going to work its magic for one of us today, I just know it,' Beth says, bright-eyed.

'Hope so,' Willow grins. 'Y'know, Daizy, it might even be you!'

I roll my eyes, but today does feel special, somehow. Maybe Paris will work its magic on me, helping me to re-create the kind of cool,

crazy colour explosions that made Jacques Genet fall in love with my red squirrel painting. I pick up the clipboard and look at it again. I can't quite see what all the fuss was about, but Jacques is the expert, after all.

I have finally found my star quality – and this time it will not go wrong, whatever Beth and Willow think. Jacques will arrive later to pick up my painting . . . and life will never be the same again. Forget the Star of the Week award, maybe I'll end up studying art in Paris! That would show Beth and Willow. Who needs Brightford Academy? Who needs lovesick friends and giant red squirrels and Ethan Miller? Not me.

Miss Moon puts her head round the bedroom door. 'Dreaming again, Daizy?' she says. 'Hurry, girls – we're meeting downstairs in five minutes! It's our last day, we don't want to waste a second of it!'

There are about
a million stairs
inside the Eiffel
Tower, but we have
queued for ages
and it is a relief to be
climbing upwards at last.
Beth and Willow haven't even
bothered to wait for me –
they raced on ahead
after Ethan Miller,
who is sprinting up
the stairs as if
he is trying
to escape.

Murphy and I struggle out on to the first viewing platform, and I take a deep breath. Paris is spread before us, a patchwork of rooftops, river and greenery. It's amazing. I'm sure I can get inspired and create a masterpiece from up here.

'We'll take a short break, Class Six,' Miss Moon tells us. 'Ten minutes . . . and then up to the next level!'

Murphy wanders away, taking photos, and Ethan Miller appears at my side. Great.

'Hide me, Daizy,' he pleads. 'Beth and Willow won't leave me alone! Every time I look round they are there, fluttering their eyelashes and flirting . . .'

'How awful for you,' I sigh.

'It's not my fault they are crushing on me, is it?' he shrugs. 'I didn't ask them to! I mean, obviously, they have excellent taste . . .'

'You are the vainest, most annoying boy I have ever met,' I huff.

'You like me really,' Ethan smirks. 'I can tell!'

'You really can't,' I say. 'Trust me on that.'

Beth and Willow rush up and link arms with Ethan. 'There you are!' they gush. 'We've been looking for you! Isn't this the best view in the whole world? Isn't it romantic?'

Ethan smiles in a slightly alarmed kind of way, but I have no sympathy. I walk away, leaving Ethan to his fate, and a few minutes later Miss Moon has us climbing upwards again. It's even more of a slog this time, but once on the second

viewing platform we barely stop to catch our breath before Miss Moon herds us towards the glass-walled elevators. The doors slide closed behind us.

'Ethan!' Beth is saying. 'I'm scared of heights! Stay with me!'

'I can't look!' Willow yelps, burying her face in Ethan's shoulder.

We begin the ascent to the very top, and although my tummy flips over once or twice, I don't feel the urge to squeal and clutch on to anyone's sleeve. I am way too excited for that. The lift whooshes to a halt and we swarm out on to the final viewing platform, higher than I have ever been before.

When you have seen Paris from the top of the Eiffel Tower, you know you can do anything. I feel literally on top of the world. I can see my life spread out around me, beautiful and slightly distant, like the Parisian landscape. I can see it all, the hopes, the dreams, the possibilities. I know that I will remember this moment forever.

'Awesome,' Murphy breathes.

'I know,' I sigh. 'It's . . . wow. Just wow.'

Then I catch sight of Ethan Miller squished in between Beth and Willow, and my heart sinks. Whenever I pictured this day, I imagined the four of us together, laughing, inseparable, forever friends. It hasn't turned out like that at all. I want to be here with my best, best friends and they have deserted me for a vain, football-mad pest who doesn't even like them all that much.

I thought that Paris would bring us all together. Instead it looks like it has broken us apart for good.

It's funny how Paris can still look so beautiful, even through a mist of tears.

Back down on the second viewing platform, Miss Moon tells us we have an hour to spend any way we like. While the rest of the class head for the café and souvenir shop, I take out my clipboard and lean on the railings, determined to make another painting for Jacques Genet.

Paris is like a huge patchwork blanket wrapped around the foot of the tower. I sketch in the winding ribbon of the River Seine, the parks, the boxy rooftops, the tracery of streets that hold it all together. The drawing pulls me in. A little bit of magic has found its way on to the page, without the help of spilt paint or paw

prints or muddy tyre tracks. This is all my own work.

I unclip yesterday's red squirrel picture, studying it. Jacques Genet wants more pictures like this, but I don't want to spill paint on today's drawing, or throw it into a puddle. I like it just the way it is.

I'm so deep in thought I don't even notice Ethan Miller sneaking up behind me to steal my beret and sunglasses.

'Ethan!' I yelp. 'What are you doing?'

'Hiding,' he says, pulling on the disguise. 'Your friends are driving me nuts. Every time I turn round, they're there –'

'You shouldn't have strung them along all this time,' I say, and Ethan snorts and says that he has spent most of the year trying not to encourage them. This may be true. Beth and Willow don't need any encouragement when it comes to Ethan.

'The thing is, I like someone else,' he sighs. 'I've been trying to let her know all year, but she doesn't seem to notice me at all.'

'Sensible girl.'

'I'm not sure she is sensible,' Ethan considers. 'But she is definitely very kind and very cute and quite eccentric.'

He peers at me over the rims of the stolen sunglasses, his blue eyes smouldering. I wonder if he has spotted a spider on my hair, or possibly a stray crumb from my breakfast croissant, but then he winks and grins at me, and I panic. Ethan Miller is not very bright, but surely he couldn't actually be foolish enough to fall for ME?

Sadly, with Ethan, you have to expect the worst.

'Daizy,' he whispers. 'You are the only girl for me!'

My blood runs cold. This is a disaster, a nightmare! I want to run away, but I'm halfway up a really tall tower, and totally trapped. Great.

'I am actually not the only girl for you,' I tell Ethan briskly. 'At all!'

'You are!' he insists. 'It's fate!'

I feel cold all over, as if someone has poured leftover nettle soup down my neck. I mean, seriously? Why me? What have I done to deserve this?

'It's so not fate,' I say. 'In case you haven't noticed, Ethan, I am immune to your so-called charms. I am not interested in you. Not. One. Single. Bit.'

His face lights up. 'I know!' he gushes. 'It's amazing! I think that's why I have fallen for you, Daizy Star. I like a challenge!'

'It's not a challenge, it's an impossibility,' I tell him. 'Why not go for Beth or Willow? They actually seem to like you, though I can't think why . . .'

Ethan laughs. 'I don't care about Beth or Willow,' he says. 'I like YOU. Please give me a chance!'

'Never,' I huff.

The full horror of Ethan's announcement begins to unfold in my mind. The boy my friends are crushing on has fallen for me . . . this is a disaster, a car crash, a full-on nightmare. My friendship with Beth and Willow is on the rocks as it is. Once they find out about this, the shipwreck will be complete. They may never speak to me again.

Ethan shoots me a sly grin and snatches the exploding-squirrel picture from my hands, waving it high above his head.

'C'mon!' he teases. 'Be my girlfriend and I'll keep your dad's dodgy job a secret. OK? Otherwise . . . well, I might just happen to tell everyone that

he is actually a giant red squirrel.'

'That's blackmail!' I howl. 'Give me that picture back!'

I lunge forward to rescue my masterpiece just as Ethan leans in, planting a wet, sloppy kiss on my ear. It is traumatic, like when you're little and your mum comes at you unawares with a warm, soapy flannel, only much scarier. If this is romance, you can keep it.

I make a grab at the squirrel picture just as Ethan tugs it back, out of reach. There is a loud tearing noise as the painting rips, and Ethan drops it in a panic. The wind whips the torn

pieces up into the air, and I watch in horror as they drift above the barbed-wire safety barrier and float away on the breeze.

'Noooooo!' I screech. 'My PAINTING!'

I watch, helpless, as my accidental masterpiece flutters down through the air and is eventually lost to sight among the Parisian rooftops.

'Oops,' Ethan says in a small voice. In just a few hours' time, gallery owner Jacques Genet is coming to collect my red squirrel masterpiece, which is probably even now lying in pieces in a gutter somewhere. My life is over.

'I wouldn't really have told anyone your red squirrel secret,' Ethan says.

'I don't care any more,' I tell him. 'Yes, my dad dresses up in a red squirrel suit. Is that a problem? He is my dad, and I love him, no matter what!'

Ethan tugs the beret down over his forehead. 'So . . . I suppose a date would be out of the question?' he asks.

'Yes, Ethan, it would,' I huff. 'No date. Not

now, not tomorrow, not EVER. Understand? And yes, my dad has a very weird job, but is that a crime? Is that a joke? No, Ethan, it is NOT!'

He looks slightly alarmed now, but I am fizzing with anger and I cannot stop.

'MY DAD IS A GIANT RED SQUIRREL,' I yell at the top of my voice, and tourists turn to stare at me, baffled. 'SO WHAT? I AM VERY PROUD OF HIM, OK?'

'I know,' Murphy says, running over to my side. 'It's OK, Daizy.'

Beth and Willow appear, and my heart sinks. Did they see Ethan flirting, chatting me up . . . ? Ethan trying to kiss me? They'll be furious. I wait, resigned, for the explosion.

It doesn't come.

'Your dad is great, Daizy,' Beth says kindly. 'Of course you're proud of him.'

Willow slides an arm round me. 'We've known about the squirrel thing for ages, y'know. We just didn't mention it because YOU didn't. Thought you might want to keep it quiet.'

'Who wouldn't?' Ethan Miller muses, and Beth and Willow turn on him.

'Ethan, go AWAY!' Beth growls, grabbing the beret and sunglasses and handing them back to me. 'Haven't you done enough?'

'We saw,' Willow adds. 'We saw EVERYTHING, Ethan, and we were not impressed. Push off and leave us alone!'

'Girls, girls, you don't mean that!' he grins.

Beth and Willow just glare, and Ethan wilts, sloping sadly away. My friends have spent a whole year crushing on this boy, only to have their dreams crash and burn, just as mine have. What amazes me is that they are right here at my side, loyal and supportive, even though they must be hurting inside. It is kind of a miracle.

Maybe our friendship is stronger than I thought?

'You were right about that boy,' Willow says scornfully.

'He's a creep,' Beth sulks. 'We were in the café and he told us to queue for some Coke and crisps, that he'd save us a seat. We couldn't find him anywhere, so we came out here to look, and . . .'

Her face crumples, and a tear rolls down her cheek.

'I don't even like him, if it's any comfort,' I say.

'We know,' Willow sighs. 'We've been stupid, Daizy. Getting all mushy about a boy . . . they're just not worth it.'

'Some of us are OK,' Murphy grins.

'Sorry, Murphy,' Willow agrees. 'Some of you are the best ever. I'm going to miss you so much at Brightford Academy, y'know.'

'Me too,' Beth says sadly. 'It just won't be the same.'

'Me, three,' I sigh.

'Well, I haven't decided yet,' Murphy tells us. 'I might still end up at Brightford Academy . . . they do have a really good art department.'

'No way!' I gasp. 'Really? Oh please, Murphy,

please, PLEASE come to Brightford!'

'It won't seem so scary if you're there,' Willow chips in, and that's the first time I've ever heard her admit she is nervous about going to secondary school. Maybe my friends aren't quite as confident as they pretend?

Murphy winks and I begin to hope that maybe, just maybe, everything will be OK after all.

'Ethan is SO not the boy I thought he was,' Willow sighs. 'He was blackmailing you, Daizy. He ripped your picture in half and threw it off the Eiffel Tower!'

'He didn't mean it,' I shrug. 'It was sort of an accident. But there's an important gallery owner coming to collect it for an exhibition later. He said it was a masterpiece of modern art – and now it's gone!'

Beth and Willow frown. 'A masterpiece? That red squirrel thing? Are you sure?'

'Very sure,' I say, a little huffily.

'We thought you were joking,' Willow blinks.

'Nope,' I sigh. 'But it's all ruined now. I've lost the picture!'

'At least you've got another one,' Murphy points out, nodding at the drawing on my clipboard. 'It's not modern art, exactly, but I think I like it better . . .'

I look at the drawing. I like it too, but I know it's not what Jacques Genet is looking for.

'Jacques won't like it,' I worry. 'There are no splashes of mud, no stuck-on grass, no cat or tyre prints, no spilt paint . . .'

'So, we'll do some like that,' Willow says. 'We'll help you, Daizy. How hard can it be?'

'We can use Pierre's studio,' Beth grins. 'It'll be fun!'

A wave of happiness swamps me. Just when I thought all was lost, my friends have come to the rescue . . . instead of losing them, I've discovered how loyal they really are. They may not understand my new star quality; they may worry that it will end in tears; but still, they are helping me to give it my very best shot.

'Teamwork,' Murphy shrugs. 'That's what friends are for!'

Miss Moon appears with a camera and we grin and wave and pose together for a photo, halfway up the Eiffel Tower, just like I always imagined we would. Perhaps it's not the end of the world after all that I lost that stupid painting?

16

We spend the afternoon in Pierre's studio shed, trying to re-create the red squirrel painting. The little white cat watches from the paint table as we splash and splatter the paint.

'I really thought you were imagining that cat,' Beth grins, planting a blue handprint in the centre of one of the paintings. 'Did you say Pierre calls her Picasso?'

'Well, she loves playing with paint,' I say. 'She's the real reason my red squirrel picture was so . . . well, weird.'

'Cool,' Willow says, wheeling Madame Le Chapeau's bicycle across the wet paintings to

re-create the tyre-print effect. 'Who knew modern art could be so much fun?'

The studio looks like the scene of a small massacre, but I'm still not sure the pictures are working.

'Something's missing,' I sigh.

'Cat prints!' Murphy says, eyeing Picasso, who is pawing at a dish of red paint.

I frown. 'It was an accident, last time. I don't think it'd be fair to make her do it. She might be scared!'

Willow narrows her eyes. 'What if we just . . . encourage her to stand in the paint and see what happens?'

Warily, I lift Picasso up and stand her in the tray of thick red paint. She unleashes a bloodcurdling howl and ricochets across the studio like a firecracker. A paint palette falls

down on top of her, streaking her with blue, orange and pink.

'Quick!' I yell. 'Catch her! She'll wreck Pierre's paintings!'

Beth dives towards the cat, misses and lands face down on the floor, while Willow's rugby tackle sends yet more paint flying. Murphy and I skid about the studio trying to grab Picasso, but every time we get close she zigzags away again, her tail puffed up like a giant paintbrush, leaving smears of colour everywhere.

'Nooooo!' I wail, the first time I see her smudge paint across one of Pierre's pictures. 'Stop, Picasso!' But she doesn't stop – she can't. She rubs herself against the finished canvasses stacked against the walls and climbs the easels, leaving ghostly streaks in rainbow colours. The more we chase, the more she runs.

'Leave her,' I say finally. 'We're scaring her. Let her calm down.'

The little cat slinks away beneath the chair in the corner, and Beth, Willow, Murphy and I

exchange horrified glances. Every one of Pierre's carefully painted pictures is smeared with paint and cat fur. I have destroyed them, with a little help from Picasso.

At that moment, the studio door swings open and Jacques Genet strides into the room, Pierre and Miss Moon at his heels.

'*Zut alors!*' Jacques exclaims. 'What is going on?'

I am in the middle of the studio, with paint streaked across my face and dripping down my arms. I see Pierre's shocked face as he takes in the carnage of his ruined pictures, and I feel more ashamed than I ever have in my life. Sometimes, I think my only star quality

is to bring doom and disaster to everyone I meet.

'Daizy is a very hands-on kind of artist,' Murphy says, stepping forward bravely. 'She likes to get her hands in the paint. And her hair. And . . . er . . . her cat.'

Jacques Genet grins. 'You've been creating more masterpieces for me?'

'That's right,' I say. 'Here they are. On the . . . er . . . floor.'

The gallery owner peers at the pictures, now all but hidden beneath a thick crust of paint and a scrum of foot and paw prints. 'Interesting,' he shrugs. 'But . . . there is no spark of genius here. I am sorry, Daizy, but I think perhaps I will just take your masterpiece from yesterday . . .'

'Right,' I whisper. 'About that. I seem to have . . . um . . . lost it.'

'Lost it?' he repeats. 'LOST it? But . . . this was a work of groundbreaking genius! You cannot just . . . LOSE it!'

'I dropped it off the Eiffel Tower,' I sigh. 'It

was in two halves by then, anyway. I think most of it ended up in the river.'

Jacques Genet hides his face in his hands.

'Hey,' Murphy says. 'Daizy has one more drawing you might like . . .' He picks up the clipboard, peeling off the paint-spattered top sheet to reveal my intricate Eiffel Tower drawing, but the gallery owner barely glances at it.

'No, no, no!' he snaps. 'Don't waste my time with this worthless nonsense!'

Tears blur my vision, but I am aware of Miss Moon stepping forward, hands on hips. 'You are a rude and foolish man,' she tells him sternly. 'You should be ashamed of yourself, raising a little girl's hopes like this and then dashing them again!'

Jacques Genet wilts under her gaze like a naughty schoolboy.

'The red squirrel picture was an accident,' I tell him. 'I tried to explain, but you wouldn't listen!'

'I needed something special for my exhibition,' he sighs. 'I thought I'd found it, but I was wrong.

If I have raised your hopes for nothing, I am sorry.' He turns away sadly, then stops short, staring at one of Pierre's ruined paintings.

Please don't let him say anything mean about it . . . that would be the last straw.

'At last!' he exclaims, his eyes scanning the artwork. 'You tried to fool me with childish jokes, but all the time your real work was waiting! You really ARE a genius, Daizy Star!'

'Huh?'

'This!' Jacques Genet says, peering at one of Pierre's canvasses. 'Your REAL work. Simple, ordinary paintings hidden beneath a random blurring of paint . . . and is that cat fur? Incredible! Amazing!'

Pierre looks at me, eyes wide. He nods towards the spoiled pictures, giving me permission to take credit for them, but I know I can't do that. I'm sick of pretending to be something I am not.

'No,' I say clearly. 'These paintings are Pierre's! Pierre is the real genius here . . .'

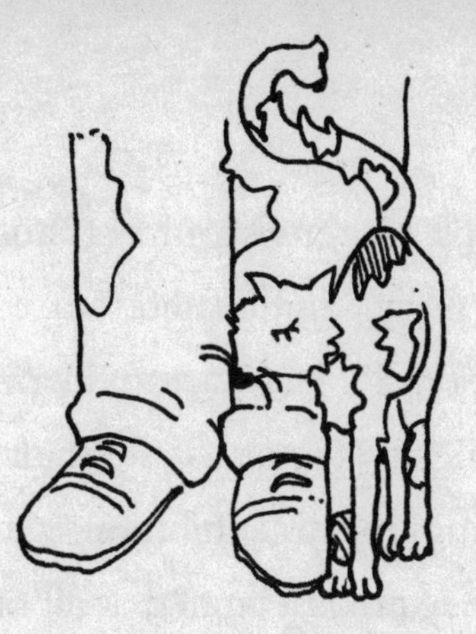

There is a miaow from the corner, and Picasso slinks out from her hiding place beneath the chair, her fur a riot of colour. She glares at me, then stalks over to Pierre and presses herself against his ankles, purring.

'Well,' I say, smiling. 'Pierre and his cat.'

I press my cheek against the cool glass of the ferry window, watching the French coastline fade into a blur of grey. '*Au revoir*, France,' I sigh, turning back to my friends.

I will never forget Paris. I didn't find my star quality after all, but I learnt lots of other things – and they are way more important. I've learnt that when your picture gets wrecked by a stray cat it's best to just say so, and not to pretend that it is a

work of genius. Otherwise, things can get complicated. Very complicated.

From now on, I'll leave art to the proper artists. Last night, Jacques Genet took Pierre's ruined paintings for his exhibition – according to Jacques, they are not ruined at all but touched by magic. Pierre said that we had brought him luck, and that Picasso the cat was going to be his 'muse' and live in the little studio forever.

'You've changed my life, Daizy Star,' he said as we waved goodbye. 'My dream has come true, thanks to you . . . and Picasso!'

And who knew that Ethan Miller could actually teach me something useful? I've learnt never to let anybody blackmail me, especially not halfway up the Eiffel Tower. It will almost certainly end in tears, or lost paintings, or sloppy kisses on the ear. Not good.

You should never, ever feel ashamed of the people you love, even if one of them does have a tendency to dress up as a giant red squirrel in

his spare time. I wasted a lot of energy trying to keep Dad's job secret when it turns out that my friends knew anyway . . . and they really didn't care.

'Parents are embarrassing,' Murphy points out. 'That's the whole point of them. Learning to handle it is a part of growing up.'

'You think so?' I check. 'Really?'

'Really,' Willow nods. 'They're all the same, Daizy. Remember the time my mum came to Parents' Evening wearing a sequinned bikini top and lemon-yellow flares, on her way to a seventies party?'

'I remember,' I say.

'Well then,' Willow sighs. 'That had to be right up there with the red squirrel suit, but I survived it, and you will survive this.'

I guess she's right. The most important thing I have learnt this trip is that nothing can ever come between me and my friends. All year I have been worried that Beth and Willow were growing up too fast, drifting away from me . . . and yesterday,

when Ethan kissed my ear and dropped my painting off the Eiffel Tower, I thought I'd lose them forever. Instead, they rescued me and they've been by my side ever since.

Maybe my mad search for a star quality has bugged them at times, just as their crush on Ethan bugged me, but none of that matters now. I am not scared that secondary school will break us apart. We'll have our ups and downs, but I know we can come through just about anything as long as we stick together. Whichever school Murphy decides on, we'll be OK. We are unbreakable.

I glance at Ethan, sitting a few tables over. He is showing off to a group of French schoolkids nearby, throwing peanuts up into the air to catch in his mouth. He looks my way, and the smile slides off his face. He manages to look sorry, for a split second at least, and then his mates distract him and he is clowning about again, shaking up a can of Coke and spraying everyone within a twenty-metre radius.

'What did I ever see in that boy?' Beth huffs. 'He's so immature!'

'I never really liked him,' Willow remarks. 'Not seriously. I just pretended I did, for your sake . . .'

'Yeah, yeah,' Beth snorts.

I bite back a grin, but I'm glad the crush is finally over. Maybe now Beth and Willow will get back to normal? Or maybe not.

Two cool French boys walk past, shooting a sly glance in our direction, and Beth and Willow blush scarlet.

'Ooh la la,' I grin, and they collapse into giggles.

17

When we get home, life gets back to normal, or as normal as it can be when your dad wears a red squirrel suit for a living. The class lists come in for Brightford Academy and, amazingly, Beth, Willow, Murphy and I are all in the same form.

'Are you definitely coming to Brightford Academy?' I ask Murphy.

'Definitely,' he says. 'Mum said it was up to me in the end, and how could I choose anywhere else? Dad wasn't keen on the arts school anyhow, and Mum didn't like the idea of all that train travel . . .'

'So, we're stuck with you,' Willow grins.

'Looks like,' he says. 'Friends forever, right?'

'Forever,' Beth agrees.

'And ever,' I add, hauling them in for a group hug.

Back at the start of the year, I had high hopes of Year Six – I thought I'd find my star quality and change the world. Somehow, now, friendship seems more important, and secondary school doesn't scare me any more, not now I know we'll be together.

'Not everyone finds their talent right away, Daizy,' Mum tells me, the evening before my last ever day at Stella Street Primary. 'I didn't know I wanted to be a nurse until I was seventeen, and your dad didn't decide to be a teacher until he was in his twenties . . .'

I decide not to mention that when Dad reached his forties he changed his mind and decided that his real talent was dressing up as a giant red squirrel. Sometimes, a star quality can go horribly wrong.

Mum puts an arm round me. 'You can do

anything you set your mind to,' she tells me. 'Dream big, Daizy, and work hard to make the dreams happen. That's what your dad has been doing this year, and although I haven't always approved of the dreams, I know it's been important for him to follow them.'

'I guess,' I say.

'Secondary school will open up a whole new bunch of possibilities,' Mum grins. 'You'll love it, Daizy, I promise!'

My last day ever at Stella Street Primary is actually the happiest and saddest day ever, all

rolled into one. There's an assembly and lots of talk about reaching for the stars, and I try very hard to smile, even though I think my heart might be breaking. I have been reaching for the stars all year, and where has it got me? Nowhere. Not even one single measly Star of the Week award.

Later, we have a classroom party and everyone signs each other's sweatshirts so we will never, ever forget this day.

Friends forever, Beth writes; *Best mate in the world*, Willow adds; *Stay cool*, Murphy scrawls. Ethan just writes *Sorry*, and I decide that, actually, it's not his fault he is the most annoying boy in the universe. Probably.

Miss Moon shuts down the music and everyone is quiet.

'This is our last day together, Class Six,' she says. 'You'll soon be moving on, taking up new challenges. I've loved being your teacher this year – I will never forget any of you.'

A fat tear rolls down my cheek. Miss Moon has brought out the best in all of us. She has given Star of the Week awards to my classmates, picking out the things that make them shine.

'You're a wonderful class,' she says proudly. 'Each and every one of you has gained my respect and admiration this year – for your hard work, your talents, your kindness. Those Star of the Week awards have been well earned.'

I swallow. I have never been singled out for one of those awards – am I the only one in the whole class not to have gained Miss Moon's respect and admiration?

'There is one pupil, however, who has stood out from all the rest,' Miss Moon is saying. 'This pupil is bright, brave, determined, imaginative . . . and always thinking of others.

I could have given her the Star of the Week award over and over again . . .'

I look around me. Could it be Beth? Willow? Sheena, perhaps?

'I have created an extra-special award for this very special person,' Miss Moon announces. 'Congratulations, Daizy Star – our very own STAR OF THE YEAR!'

An explosion of whoops and cheers erupts around me, and my heart thumps so hard I think it might burst right out of my chest.

'Go on,' Murphy nudges me, and Beth and Willow push me forward to collect my certificate.

It is printed on thick white card and edged with gold, and it is the most totally perfect thing I have ever seen in my life. I will treasure it forever.

'Thank you, Miss!' I whisper. 'Thank you so, so much!'

'You are a stand-out pupil, Daizy Star,' Miss Moon smiles. 'Your classmates agree with me on that. You've earned this award – for designing the new infant school play park, for thinking up the idea of the sponsored swim . . .'

'For conquering your fears and learning to swim,' Willow says.

'Raising money for Malawi at the Battle of the Bands,' Murphy chips in.

'Helping me when I was upset about my gran last term,' Beth adds. 'And the old people's home. And there was the way you rescued Picasso and helped Pierre to achieve his dream . . .'

'There are too many things to mention,' Miss Moon says. 'But we want you to know that we appreciate you, Daizy – you have a very starry future ahead of you!'

Just when I think it can't get any better, Miss Moon produces a huge chocolate cake covered in sparklers. 'Trust me, Class Six,' she grins. 'You are going to love Brightford Academy. And remember . . . life is sweet!'

Later, back home, I show Mum, Dad, Becca and Pixie my Star of the Year award. 'I'm going to frame it and keep it forever,' I sigh. 'This is officially the best day of my whole life!'

'You deserve it,' Pixie says. 'You are a very good big sister.'

'You're an OK little sister too,' Becca agrees.

'Dad and I have always been very proud of you, Daizy,' Mum adds. 'But it's lovely to see that your teacher and your classmates appreciate you as well. And you're right – today really is a special day. Your dad has some good news for you all too!'

We look at Dad, who is looking very happy and unusually smart in a suit and tie.

'No way . . . you've ditched the squirrel costume?' Becca guesses.

'That's certainly a part of it,' Dad grins.

I narrow my eyes, looking out of the window. 'You've sold the van!' I say. 'Finally!'

'Right again,' Dad says. 'I've handed in my notice at the Squirrel & Lentil Wholefood Café, and, yes, they've taken the van off my hands. And that's not all of it. I have had the most wonderful year, following my dreams . . . but now I am ready to go back to work full time. Not as a red squirrel, but as a teacher!'

'Yessss!' Pixie yells. 'No more squirrel tail! No more stinky van!'

'Yess!' Becca says. 'You've got your old job back, finally!'

'Better than that,' Dad explains. 'It's a new job – a promotion. And it's not at Green Lane Community School, either. Just wait till you hear. Trust me, girls, you will LOVE this . . .'

My smile freezes. I have a bad feeling about this, a very bad feeling. My dad, formerly a giant red squirrel, has landed himself a new job. That's fine. That's good. There's no need to panic. Is there?

'You are looking at the new Head of Geography at Brightford Academy,' Dad announces proudly. 'Won't that be great?'

I look at Becca, and she looks at me. Our faces struggle to hide the horror, but the more I try the harder it gets and a wild, slightly frantic laugh escapes. Pretty soon Becca is laughing too, snorting and sniggering in a very unladylike way.

There is only one thing worse than a dad who dresses in a squirrel suit, and that is a dad who teaches geography at your new secondary school.

I swallow back my giggles. According to Beth and Willow, embarrassing parents are all part of growing up. If so, I will be getting VERY grown-up, any day now.

Well, I guess that, whatever happens, Beth, Willow and Murphy will help me to cope – that's

what friends are for. Besides, I also know how important it is to follow your dreams, and it looks like teaching might be Dad's dream after all.

'Great,' I say. 'Brilliant, Dad . . . brilliant.'

And I put my arms round him and hug him tightly.

Random Acts of Kindness

Copy cool Sam Taylor from *Ginger Snaps* and try a random act of kindness every day. Here are a few to start you off . . .

- *Wash up* without being asked
- *Hug* a friend!
- *Talk* to someone who's feeling lonely or left out
- *Compliment* a classmate on his/her appearance
- *Send a card* to your BFF for no reason at all
- *Carry shopping* for an elderly neighbour
- *Play* with your little bruv/sister – it's fun!
- *Smile* – it's free, and it makes everyone feel good. Especially you!

And why not show your *BFFs* how much you care by organizing something that you could do together? The most important thing is spending time with each other and having fun!

- *Throw a mini party for your best friends* – you could all watch a DVD together, or make your own dream flags to hang in your room. Or maybe you could bake your own Angel Cakes!
- *Hold a cake sale* – once you've baked your yummy cakes, why not set up a stall to sell them? Maybe you could raise money for a charity that really means something to you.
- *Invite your friends to a clothes-swapping party* – you might not be in love with that sparkly top any more, but maybe one of your friends would look great in it. And you save money by not having to buy new clothes! Why not make it into a pamper party and spoil each other with some new hair looks?

For more ideas go to www.cathycassidy.com

How can you make your WISHES and DREAMS come TRUE?

WISHES and DREAMS are just other words for positive thinking, and that's something that can be very powerful! Get together with friends and create some beautiful dream flags to start the magic . . .

You will need:

- A3 white or coloured paper
- Coloured crayons, felt pens, oil pastels, water-based paints, brushes, scissors, glue, glitter, sequins, yarn, foil streamers, tinsel, stickers, stars, tissue paper, ribbon, gold/silver pens, assorted collage materials
- A long length of string/coloured cord/ribbon
- IMAGINATION!!!

How to make your DREAM FLAG:

- Take your piece of A3 paper and cut it in half lengthways. Then fold each piece in half so you have two long thin strips of paper. This will give you 2 flags.
- Use paints, pens, crayons, pastels or a combination to pattern/colour the paper. Or collage your flag with ribbon, foil, stars and paper.
- Write your dream on to the flag shape. If you'd rather keep the dream secret, just decorate the flag with your own patterns and symbols, but think about your dream while you are doing this.
- Use both sides of the flag, or get your friend to use the other side so you can share the dream flag!
- Fold your flag over the string/cord and staple or glue your flag into place . . . then hang the dream flags along a wall or classroom!

How to make your very own friendship bracelets

Friendship bracelets are great fun to make, and even better to make with and for your best friend! There are lots of colours and patterns you can use to create a unique and special bracelet for your friend.

Method 1: The easiest way to make a friendship bracelet is by plaiting.

1. Choose 3 colours of thread that you like.
2. Take 2 strands of each colour.
3. Tie a knot in the end of the 6 strands and separate the different colours from each other.
4. Get your friend to hold the knotted end of the bracelet and start plaiting the 3 colours together.
5. Once the bracelet is long enough to go around your wrist, tie a knot in the other end.
6. Snip off any straggly ends and you're done!

Method 2: This is more difficult but you'll end up with a cool pattern.

1. Take 6 strands of thread – choose any colours you like.
2. Each strand represents a letter in the word **FRIEND**.
3. Tie a knot in the end of the 6 strands.

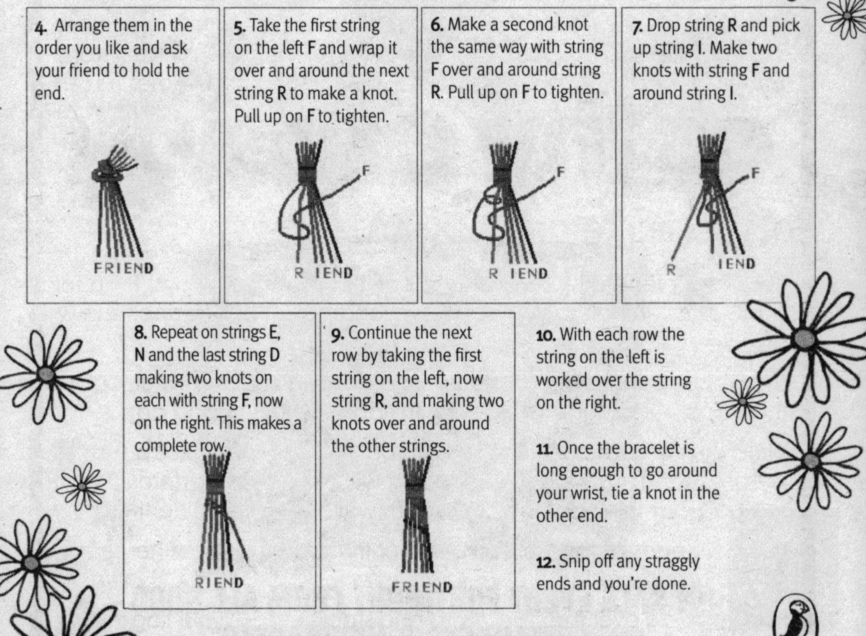

4. Arrange them in the order you like and ask your friend to hold the end.
5. Take the first string on the left **F** and wrap it over and around the next string **R** to make a knot. Pull up on **F** to tighten.
6. Make a second knot the same way with string **F** over and around string **R**. Pull up on **F** to tighten.
7. Drop string **R** and pick up string **I**. Make two knots with string **F** and around string **I**.
8. Repeat on strings **E**, **N** and the last string **D** making two knots on each with string **F**, now on the right. This makes a complete row.
9. Continue the next row by taking the first string on the left, now string **R**, and making two knots over and around the other strings.
10. With each row the string on the left is worked over the string on the right.
11. Once the bracelet is long enough to go around your wrist, tie a knot in the other end.
12. Snip off any straggly ends and you're done.

www.cathycassidy.com

She's quirky and cool and loving life with her best friends Willow and Beth

A fab and funny series starring Daizy

Perfect for your little sister, or as a mini read for you!

It all started with a Scarecrow.

Puffin is seventy years old.

Sounds ancient, doesn't it? But Puffin has never been so lively. We're always on the lookout for the next big idea, which is how it began all those years ago.

Penguin Books was a big idea from the mind of a man called Allen Lane, who in 1935 invented the quality paperback and changed the world. **And from great Penguins, great Puffins grew, changing the face of children's books forever.**

The first four Puffin Picture Books were hatched in 1940 and the first Puffin story book featured a man with broomstick arms called Worzel Gummidge. In 1967 Kaye Webb, Puffin Editor, started the Puffin Club, promising to **'make children into readers'**. She kept that promise and over 200,000 children became devoted Puffineers through their quarterly instalments of *Puffin Post*, which is now back for a new generation.

Many years from now, we hope you'll look back and remember Puffin with a smile. **No matter what your age or what you're into, there's a Puffin for everyone.** The possibilities are endless, but one thing is for sure: whether it's a picture book or a paperback, a sticker book or a hardback, **if it's got that little Puffin on it – it's bound to be good.**